About the Author

Amit Chaudhuri is the multi-award-winning author of six critically acclaimed novels. He is a Fellow of the Royal Society of Literature and Professor of Contemporary Literature at the University of East Anglia.

Praise for *Odysseus Abroad*

'He has beautifully practiced a "refutation of the spectacular" throughout his career, both as a novelist and as a critic ... Rich with hanging vignettes of domestic and urban life; the atmosphere is impressionistic, poetic, softly comic ... Radhesh and Ananda represent two generations in what Naipaul called "that great movement of peoples that was to take place in the second half of the twentieth century." Each immigrant deals with the loss of his home, and the quest for a new one, in his own way.'   James Wood, *The New Yorker*

'A little gem not to be missed ... In the eccentric Radhesh, Chaudhuri gives us something special.'   *Daily Mail*

'Audacious ... Chaudhuri's luminously intelligent novel appropriates a literary tradition that is both his and not his; in making Homer and Joyce speak in Bengali and in the English used by educated, cosmopolitan Bengalis, *Odysseus Abroad* has placed itself, with erudition and playfulness, on the map of modernism.'   Neel Mukherjee, *Guardian*

'Apart from its comedic delights, this playfully allusive novel, with its echoes of Joyce and Homer, offers eloquent meditations on family and the fracturing of identity.'   *New York Times*

'Chauduri's writing is so fresh and immediate, and often powerfully observant ... He paints the background with a light, sure hand, recreating the atmosphere of London in those post-Falkland days when Mrs Thatcher seemed set to rule for ever.'   Kate Saunders, *The Times*

'Chaudhuri is a singular writer. He defies form; instead he has perfected an observational fiction based on insight and memory ... witty, effortlessly fluid ... a pleasure to read.'   Eileen Battersby, *Irish Times*

'The novel ... n two cultures build them ... s.'

'A brilliantly delicate London novel … an absolutely wonderful book.' *The Idler*

'A tender and wryly humorous exploration of a young man's dreams and aspirations so far from home, probing identity, race, the sadness and allure of loneliness, poignant inter-generational friendship, and the importance of companionship.' *Independent*

'A wonderful novel which has everything in it – pathos, humour, lyricism and style – by one of the most remarkable novelists writing today.' Nadeem Aslam

'Both moving and witty … This deftness and lightness of touch high-light Chaudhuri's subtle understanding of Indian life and preoccupations, particularly within the diaspora.' *Financial Times*

'Subtly questions the concept of cultural tradition … a reader with classical knowledge will enjoy the myriad Odyssean correspondences. Some small details particularly thrill.' *Daily Telegraph*

'Richly allusive … It is not the novel's plot, but its rhythmic prose, inter-woven with musical and poetical references, that most engages … a witty narrative filled with wandering and wondering.' *Observer*

'Chaudhuri's feast, a luminous and witty celebration of immigrant life, speaks to anyone who has searched for a place to call home.' *Toronto Star*

'A beautifully written novel that weaves in Indian history with a fabulously observed portrait of 1980s migrant London.' *Metro*

'A brilliantly incisive and delectably witty improvisation on Homer's *Odyssey* (which Ananda hasn't "bothered to read") and James Joyce's *Ulysses* (which Ananda found incomprehensible).' *Booklist*

'A stunningly engaging novel where Naipaul meets Amis and Joyce visits Thatcher's England. Wittingly inventive, deeply moving, it's Chaudhuri's finest work to date.' Caryl Phillips

'A superb book, one of Chaudhuri's very best – full of wit, charm and humanity, and so delicately and intricately written.' Ian Jack

'Stunning … This is his wittiest and also his most profound book to date.' Wendy Doniger

Odysseus
Abroad

Amit
Chaudhuri

ONEWORLD

A Oneworld Book

First published in Great Britain and the Commonwealth by
Oneworld Publications, 2015
This paperback edition published by Oneworld Publications in 2015

ISBN 978-1-78074-744-6
ISBN 978-1-78074-622-7 (eBook)

Printed and bound in Great Britain by Clays Ltd, St Ives plc

Oneworld Publications
10 Bloomsbury Street
London WC1B 3SR
England

In Baba's memory, with gratitude and love
And for Rinka, who wanted this book

Contents

'. . . I have tried to be as faithful to my recollections as I possibly could be. No doubt the unreliability and capriciousness of memory have led me to run together certain incidents and occasions, and to confuse some of the people involved in them. But if I have done these things, they have been done inadvertently. At no point have I deliberately departed from what I remember, or believe I remember.

At the same time . . . I wanted not only to tell the truth, as far as I knew it, about experiences I had been through or people with whom I had been involved, but also to produce tales, real stories, narratives which would provoke the reader's curiosity and satisfy it; which would appear to begin naturally, develop in a surprising and persuasive manner, and come to an end no sooner or later than they should.'

—Dan Jacobson, *Time and Time Again*

'As for these changes in me, they are the work of the warrior goddess Athene, who can do anything, and makes me look as she wishes, at one moment like a beggar and at the next like a young man finely dressed. It is easy for the gods in heaven to make or mar a man's appearance.'

—Homer, *The Odyssey*

'I believe our tradition is all of Western culture, and I also believe we have a right to this tradition, greater than that which the inhabitants of one or the other Western nation might have.'

—Jorge Luis Borges, 'The Argentine Writer and Tradition'

1

Bloody Suitors!

He got up at around nine o'clock with the usual feeling of dread. He threw off the duvet. Still unused to being vertical, he pounded the pillow and the sheet to ensure he'd dislodged strands of hair as well as the micro-organisms that subsisted on such surfaces but were invisible to the naked eye. He straightened the duvet, tugging at it till it was symmetrical on each side. He smoothed the sheet, patting it but skimming the starchy bit—a shiny patch of dried semen, already quite old—on the right flank of where he'd lain.

The anger inside him hadn't gone—from the aftermath of the concert. He'd watched it six days ago on TV: Africa, London, and Philadelphia conjoined by satellite. He switched it off after three quarters of an hour. By the time the Boomtown Rats came on, and the sea of dancing people in Wembley Stadium was being intercut with Ethiopian children with innocent eyes and bulbous heads, a phrase had arisen in his consciousness: 'Dance of death'. Didn't the exulting crowds in Wembley and in Philadelphia see their heroes' and their own complicity in the famine? But surely this line of thought was absurd, maybe malicious, and to interpret in

3

such terms an event of messianic goodwill, meant to bring joy and food to Ethiopia, nothing but perverse? So what if it brings a bit of joy to Londoners as well? Is that what you're resenting? He'd discussed it with Mark while having lunch in the Students Union Building; and Mark, in the incredibly tolerant way of one who's brushed aside death (he was a cancer survivor; his lower left leg was amputated), and who saw his friend's madness for what it was, said with self-deprecating reasonableness: 'I think *any* kind of effort that brings relief to Africa is all right.' 'Can one make an aesthetic objection, though, however awful that might sound?' Ananda had insisted. 'Can an aesthetic objection go beyond what might seem morally right? That all those people cheering and dancing in Wembley Stadium, all of them thinking that by dancing to the music they were doing those starving children a good turn—that it made it quite wrong and macabre somehow, especially when you saw the faces of the children?' Mark smiled a smile of understanding—and of one who knew death's proximity. As for Ananda: his own position on this matter underlined to him his isolation from the world—from London, for that matter.

*

That feeling had come to him at other times, when he'd seen the necessity for certain actions and yet couldn't participate in them—including the great march that took place a couple of years ago soon after he'd arrived here as a student. He remembered his first awkward hour in the college— joining the other first years for the freshers' get-together in the Common Room on the second floor of Foster Court, ascending the stairs under a painting by Whistler, and ending up informing a bespectacled girl with a Princess Di haircut that the Sanskrit *prem* meant both carnal desire and love, that there was no separation between the two in 'Indian culture'. The girl had smiled distantly. Only a week or two after his arrival, the news of the imminent cruise missiles had gathered force, leading finally to the march. He didn't want to die and he didn't want the world to blow up (as it seemed it any day would), but he couldn't spend too much time thinking of the shadow of death hanging over mankind. Yet he didn't quite admit this to himself. It was his uncle, who'd come to see him the next day in Warren Street, who'd said, while watching the Hyde Park-bound procession on TV with Monsignor Kent in the foreground (a touch of revolutionary glamour it gave to this man, the word 'Monsignor'):

'They're not getting to the root cause. They're concerned about the symptom.'

This was uttered in the droopy-eyed, amused way in which he spoke aphorisms containing a blindingly obvious truth ignored by everybody.

'Symptom?' said Ananda, challenging his uncle, but part of him chiming in.

'The nuclear bomb's only a symptom,' repeated his uncle,

almost contemptuous. 'Getting rid of it won't solve anything. Arrey baba, they have to look at the root cause.'

*

He pottered about for three or four minutes, making wasted journeys in the room, before parting the curtains and lifting the window a crack. In crumpled white kurta and pyjamas, he looked out on the street and on Tandoor Mahal opposite, unconcerned about being noticed by passers-by below. It was striking how, with the window even marginally open—heavy wooden windows he had to heave up or claw down, and which he was unused to (they made him fear for his fingers)—sounds swam into the studio flat, making him feel paradoxically at home. His mind was elsewhere. He was aware that the house itself was very quiet. The only time there was a sound was when he walked about, and a floorboard groaned at the footfall.

Upstairs, they'd sleep till midday or later. He knew when they were awake because of the sporadic bangs and thuds that announced movement. It was as if the person who first woke up didn't just get on their feet, but stamped on the floor. The noise they made wasn't intentional—it was incidental. It wasn't directed against others because it bore no awareness of others. It was pure physical expression, made by those whose heads didn't carry too many thoughts—at least, not when they woke and became mobile again.

* * *

He hadn't slept well. This was the norm; partly, it was the recurrent hyperacidity, which had him prop up two pillows against the wall—that made it difficult to sleep too—and, cursing, reach in the dark for the slim packs of Double Action Rennie he kept at his bedside. The taste of the tablets—with associations of chalk powder and spearmint—stayed with him slightly longer than their palliative effects.

But mainly it was the neighbours. They hardly slept till 3 or 4 a.m. There were three people upstairs, but also, often, a fourth. Vivek Patel, who wore pleated trousers and was lavish with aftershave; he wore accessories too—chains around the wrist, fancy belts etcetera. He had a lisp—or not a lisp, really, but a soft way of saying his t's that was both limpid and menacing. His girlfriend Cynthia stayed in the same room. She was Bengali, but from a family of Christian converts. Cynthia Roy. She was pretty and a little cheap-looking, with her bright red lipstick and simper and the thick outline of kohl, and with her sheep-like devotion to Vivek. Cynthia was a new kind of woman—a social aspirant, like her boyfriend— that Ananda couldn't really fathom, especially the mix of characteristics: newfangled but unintellectual, independent but content to be Vivek's follower. Anyway, Ananda barely existed for her. Someone had said she liked 'tough men'. Vivek wasn't taller than five feet seven or eight, but he was probably tough—because he was broad. In spite of his chains and aftershave, he had a swift, abstracted hammerhead air. Ananda had overheard him say 'Fuck off, fuck off' to Walia, the landlord, after the payphone incident—uttering the admonishment in his calm musical manner ('Fukko, fukko') to which Walia clearly had no answer. Walia had nevertheless reclaimed the payphone coin box and carried it downstairs and out of 16 Warren Street. But in all other ways he was toothless before Vivek Patel because Vivek's father, an East African businessman, was an old contact of Walia's. Patel Senior lived in Tanzania. From there, he'd sent forth two sons, Vivek and Shashank (who stayed in the single room next to his older brother), to study at the American Management School in London. Shashank looked like Vivek in a narrow mirror: he was slightly taller, paler, and a bit nicer. He spoke with the same lisp—which could have been a hallmark of Tanzanian Gujaratis. On his lips, it sounded guileless and reassuring. He'd told Ananda in the solemn way of one gripped and won over by a fiction that the American Management School offered genuine American degrees. This was the first time they'd discussed education and pretended to be high-minded students of a similar kind—to have different aims that somehow nobly overlapped and converged in this location, despite the signals to the contrary. *No wonder they don't have to study. Besides, who comes to London to do management?*

* * *

The dull pulse-like beat started at eleven o'clock at night. It was a new kind of music called 'rap'. It baffled Ananda even more than disco. He had puzzled and puzzled over why people would want to listen and even move their bodies to an angry, insistent onrush of words—words that rhymed, apparently, but had no echo or afterlife. It was as if they were an extension of the body: never had words sounded so alarmingly physical, and pure physicality lacks empathy, it's machine-like. So it seemed from his prejudiced overhearings. But down here he couldn't hear the words—only the beat and the bass note. It wasn't loud, but it was profound, and had a way of sinking through the ceiling into his body below. Each time it started, his TV was still on, and he'd allow himself to think, 'It's OK, it's not so bad really, I don't know why I let it bother me. I can ignore it.' This gave him great reassurance for a few minutes. But the very faintness of the pulse, and the way it caused the remotest of tremors—so remote he might be imagining it—was threatening.

He could cope with it while the lights were on; he could see it in perspective (how do you see a sound?) as one among other things. When he switched off the bedside lamp, the faraway boom became ominous. Its presence was absolute, interior, and continuous, erasing other noises. In a darkness outlined by the perpetual yellow light coming in through the curtains, he waited for sleep. But more than sleep, he waited for the next sound. That vigil subsumed questions that came to him intermittently, and which lacked the immediacy of *When will they turn down the music?*—questions like, What am I doing in London? And what'll I do once I'm back in India? What do I do if I don't get a First; will a 2:1 suffice? Of course I won't get a First—no one does. When will the *Poetry Review* send me a reply? I've read the stuff they publish—chatty verses are the norm—and they should be struck (at least some lonely editor tired of sifting through dry, knowing poems by English poets) by my anguish and music. Such thoughts occurred to him during the day but were now set aside in the interests of following—in addition to the bass beat—the movements upstairs. These were abrupt and powerful, as they were when the Patels first woke up at midday, and separated by typical longeurs of silence—and immobility. The gaps were excruciating, because it was then that Ananda concentrated hardest, avidly trying to decide if activity had ended for the night. By now the music would be so faint that he'd have to strain to hear the dull electronic heartbeat. But strain is what he wanted to do; to devote, eyes shut, his whole imagination to this exercise.

*

It was odd. He hadn't realised till he moved to this flat that floorboards could be so porous; and that this perviousness was an established feature of English coexistence. 'But we were colonised by them,' he thought. 'How is it that our cities are so different? How come I'm so little prepared for here?' He briefly sought but couldn't find a connection between London and Bombay—except, of course, the red double-decker buses and postboxes. It made him ill at ease—over and above having to swallow the insult of having been ruled by this nation! A nation now in turmoil, with Arthur Scargill browbeating television anchors, and the indomitable grocer's daughter unleashing policemen on horses on the miners. Ananda himself was barely aware that it was all over, that the red-faced Scargill's time was up, and that his refrain, 'At the end of the day', had caught up with him sooner than you'd have guessed two years ago. Ananda was disengaged from Indian politics but dilettantishly addicted to British politicians—the debates; the mock outrage; the amazing menu of accents; the warmth of Tony Benn's s's and his inexorable fireside eloquence; the way he cradled his pipe; the wiry trade union leaders, blown into the void by Mrs Thatcher's booming, unbudging rebuttals. It was a great spectacle, British politics——and the actual participants and the obligatory ways in which they expressed disagreement ('That is the most ridiculous tosh I've ever heard'; 'Excuse me, but I belong to a family that's been working class for generations') was even more entertaining than the moist nonsense that their Spitting Image counterparts regularly sputtered.

*

Class! He'd hardly been aware of it before coming to England—which was not so much an indication that it didn't exist in India as of the fact that the privileged were hardly conscious of it, as they were barely conscious of history—because they didn't dream they were inhabiting it, so much did they take it for granted. History was what had happened; class was something you read about in a book. Living in London, he was becoming steadily conscious of it, and not only of race, which was often uppermost in his mind. Who had spoken of the 'conscience of my race'? He couldn't remember. It sounded like a bogus formulation—probably some British orator, some old fart, maybe Winston Churchill. Then again, maybe not. Could it be a poet? Poets said the oddest things—odd for poets, that is. He'd discovered that the words he'd ascribed to some populist sloganeer and even, unconsciously, to Marx actually belonged to 'A Defence of Poetry'; there, Shelley had proclaimed: 'The rich have become richer, the poor have become poorer; and the vessel of the State is driven between the Scylla and Charybdis of anarchy and despotism.' How astute of Shelley to have noticed; and to have made that throwaway observation well before Marx made his advent into London! Marx had come here in 1846, and Shelley's Defence was published in 1840, belatedly, nineteen years after it was composed; had the bearded one noticed it, picked it up, investigated—did Marx read poetry? Did he like poets? Certainly, it appeared to Ananda that, in England now, the rich had suddenly become richer—but he could be wrong; he was no good at economics; his sights were set on the Olympian, the Parnassian: especially getting published in *Poetry Review*. He had a notion that the poor were becoming poorer, though he didn't connect this with the pit closures. His uncle had been made redundant. Serves him right. Poor man. But, if you thought about it, there was money about and people were celebrating it, the pubs in central London near his studio flat looked less despondent and ruffianly, they'd become smarter, even the curry as a consequence of this new financial self-confidence was in ascendancy, not the old spicy beef curry and rice he'd tasted first when he'd visited London as a child, nor even the homemade Indian food that left smells in hallways which white-skinned neighbours complained of, but a smart new acceptable curry, integer of the city's recent commercial success and boom. Even before he'd journeyed to England this time, to start out as a student, he'd heard that money was flowing in from North Sea Oil. Lucky bastards. Lucky for Thatcher—like a gift to her from Poseidon, or whoever the appropriate god was (he was poor in Greek mythology). Poseidon had also given her a hand at the Falklands, a war the British should have lost if only because they were British—he was angry about that. Lucky island, with more than its fair share of windfalls, rewards, and fortune. In his own land, all three million square kilometres of it, they'd dug and drilled but couldn't find a single vein of oil there, nor in the oceans surrounding its deceptively plump finger-like largely with remonstrances, seen him as a bit of a loafer, and that he, buoyed up by the British pound (even though he'd recently been made redundant), was now helping them. 'The reason I didn't marry,' he claimed in one of his monologues, 'was because *I*—he patted his frail chest lightly—'wanted to be there for my family.' *That's not entirely true. You are, and always have been, afraid of women.* Now Ananda's father made all those payments to those remote towns in the hills; the equivalent amount was transferred monthly from Ananda's uncle's National Westminster account to Ananda's. In this manner, FERA (Foreign Exchange Regulations Act) was subverted but not exactly flouted, and Ananda's low-key, apparently purposeless education was made possible. It was an arrangement that both satisfied and exacerbated his uncle. His aristocratic urge to preside and dispense—trapped within his slight five-foot-eight-inch frame—was appeased, but his precious need for privacy (he was a bachelor, after all) was compromised.

Because of the paucity of money at any given time (though Ananda didn't consciously think himself poor; he'd been born into comfort, and, since affluence is a state of mind, he possessed a primal sense of being well-off), Ananda had to ration his recurrent expenditure on lunch, dinner, books, and pornographic magazines. The last comprised all he knew at this moment of coitus. They were a let-down. He anyway suffered from a suspicion that the women were only pretending to enjoy sex, and this consciousness was a wedge between him and his own enjoyment. He required pornography to be a communal joy, shared equally between photographer, participant, and masturbator. But his suspicion was reinforced by Thatcher's repression of the hardcore. The men's penises, if you glimpsed them, were limp. There was hardly anything more innately biological and morosely unsightly than a limp penis. Meanwhile, the women's mouths were open as they lay back in their artificial rapture. Nevertheless, he pursued his climax doggedly and came on the bedsheet.

Last night, he'd brought home the first of his two customary Chinese dinner options—mixed fried rice and Singapore noodles—from the restaurant on Euston Road. The other side of that road was so still and dark (notwithstanding the sabre-like hiss of passing cars) that it might have been the sea out there for all he knew. By day, an unfriendly glass-fronted building reflected the rays of the English sun; neighbouring it was a post office. Whenever he was in the Chinese restaurant for his fried rice or Singapore noodles in the evening, it was as if these were a figment of his imaginings—until he'd seen them both the next day when he crossed the road to Euston Square. The restaurant last night had been almost empty, and the staff were as distant as ever and didn't let on that they were familiar by now with him and his order (both the Singapore rice noodles and the fried rice were one pound fifty) and with his timorous aloneness. They hardly made any attempt at conversation; presumably because their vocabulary was so austerely functional. England and its tongue refused to rub off on the staff of London's Chinese restaurants, Ananda had noticed; they continued to be defined by a dour but virginal Chineseness. Their taciturn nature was a kind of solace. Thus, silence characterised the time of waiting during which a man rushed ingredients into a wok, producing a hiss and a piercing galvanising aroma that Ananda relished as he ate in solitude, watching Question Time.

The small amount of money in his wallet meant he had to choose from an exceptionally narrow range of orders; but he didn't mind, because he mostly lacked appetite. The walk from Warren Street to the unexpected moonscape of Euston Road and back again, by when the Patels were stirring in expectation of the night, was so full of loneliness that it couldn't even be softened by self-pity. During the day, he sometimes forgot lunchtime, delaying eating since it was a boring duty, as sleeping and occasionally waking were. *What exactly should I do today? It's going to be my final year*; the hunger came and then passed, it had disappeared even from his memory, he saw it was an entirely dispensable thing he could cast aside with impunity if he ignored its birth pangs, and at half past three he bit into a green apple. For this reason, he'd grown—to his own abetting approval—very thin (poets were seldom plump) and more and more reliant upon Double Action Rennie, the acidity habitually returning to him at night-time with its stabbing pain. Still, none of these compared, in their undermining, of the stripping of his identity itself. None of the things that defined him—that he was a modern Bengali and Indian, with a cursory but proud knowledge of Bengali literature; that he wrote in English, and had spoken it much of his life; that he used to be served lettuce sandwiches as a teatime snack as a child; that in his early teenage years he'd subsisted on a diet of Agatha Christie and Earl Stanley Gardner; that he'd developed a taste for corduroys over jeans recently—almost none of this counted for anything in London, since everyone here spoke English, ate sandwiches, they wore jeans or corduroys. In this way, his identity had been taken away from him; and he'd become conscious, in England, of class. Class was what formed you, but didn't travel to other cultures—it became invisible abroad. In foreign places, you were singled out by religion and race, but not class, which was more indecipherable than any mother tongue. He'd learnt that not only were light, language, and weather contingent—class was too.

*

A sunny day! Again! One end of his white kurta fluttered in the mild breeze that was coming through the crack he'd created by pushing up the window. Almost directly opposite was Tandoor Mahal, with its unprepossessing plastic sign. Its day had begun too, though its real day would start at half past twelve, when the board on the door would be flipped on its back to say Open. He looked at it. Sunlit, like all else in the world. Lace curtains drawn, cheap red curtains tied on the sides with a sash, the menu card showing.

18

his eyes feasted on the red lacquering. But the Tandoor Mahal bird was less than ordinary. He'd gone in there earlier this year with his uncle. By then, the oozing proprietor was somehow aware they were of Sylheti ancestry, and addressed his uncle in that tongue, 'Aain, aain', a dialect his uncle abhorred—almost embracing them in his eagerness. Then, in this familial vein, he'd given them, as fellow Sylhetis, reluctant though they were, a tour of the kitchen in the basement, where the cook's helper, unmotivated and unhurried, was frying poppadum in a pan of frothy, orange oil. It was early evening, they were the only customers, and Ananda's uncle and he were pampered like honoured guests. Sylhetis behaved thus—these people, who'd single-handedly recreated this menu, this cuisine, and invented these restaurants—they distributed nourishment to the English in general (tandoori tikka masala, tarka daal, vindaloo, poppadums), but to long-sundered kin from their own land (that is, to Hindus) they extended a hand of familiarity and kindness. In their own land, Ananda's uncle and the proprietor Alam's kind had been as strangers are; then they'd contested the referendum, and his uncle, his parents, and their ilk had found themselves outnumbered and had to depart their homes altogether. But here, in these restaurants, that bitterness was forgotten, and the Sylhetis unfailingly gave them—once they discovered his uncle hailed from Bejura in Habiganj district—a chicken jhalfrezi on the house, or unobtrusively omitted the gulab jamun from the bill. Often there'd be an extra mint chocolate on the platter. The old wars were set aside; there was only compassion, transmuted from memory. The Sylhetis were great samaritans—especially to a displaced member of the race who was now without a real home in London; or so Ananda felt, instinctively, in the interiors of these restaurants. Still, the slivers of onion, the popaddum and mango chutney, the chicken tikka that Mr Alam had served them had—it was undeniable—a stale aftertaste; his uncle and he made the extra effort as they lied to Mr Alam about the food, but that was their last visit.

*

He loved light—London had taught him this fact. University had taught him little in comparison; his main education in England was imparted by the day itself, his phases of awkwardness and happiness in its fourteen or fifteen hours, and, as a result, the realisation that he adored light—*and* sound. And by sound it was the street he meant, flowing inside in a shallow current through the crack beneath the raised windowpane. *Not* the muffled bassline that could be heard from upstairs at midnight, or the Patels' abrupt forays into what must be the kitchen or the bathroom, or even Mandy playing the radio below: he didn't like interiority, or neighbours, they were too close, like the thoughts in his head. Indeed, his uncle had said to him recently when he was complaining again about the Patels: 'The noise is in your head. Stop thinking about it.' Yes, that was it: it was thought,

self-consciousness, and concentration he hated, because
they brought him back to himself, just as the sounds above
did; it was his consciousness, himself, he was often keeping
a reluctant vigil for. The silence in the studio flat when the
window was down, the silence of the library or when he was
at home reading, the lecturer's voice in a hall, they all did the
same thing too: emphasised the leaden permanence of that
proximity—the proximity of this shadowy, indestructible
thing, the self. He'd become fully aware of its constant
nearness in England. He was married to his consciousness
forever and ever. He wanted to escape, to slip away from the
'I' surreptitiously, leaving it behind somewhere. And only the
street with its sounds and manifold associations, filtering in
through the raised window on a summer's day—when but
on a summer's day could you raise a pane?—scattered and
dispelled his vigil, distracting him.

* * *

in Ananda's head even in the midst of the unpleasantness:
'So this is how it is for those who live in slums and chawls in
Bombay—this is why you hear them shouting in the middle
of the night—but worse, of course.' Ananda's mother told
Vishal he must wipe the floor clean. Vishal said, 'I never did
anything. Tell *him* to clean it up,' gesturing with his head to
Ananda. The temerity! You could see the astonishment on
his mother's face. Her son, brought up to be a prince, with
servants to keep him from lifting a finger or performing an
unnecessary chore! Would he have to do Vishal's bidding?
Then his uncle turned up, full of a glowering resentment
towards his mother (he could never quite forgive her for not
being his chattel), and began playing the fool. 'Do as he says,'
he advised solemnly, while they stood undecided before Vishal
and his mother, who was there too, supporting her son in her
obdurate ghostly way. 'Never go into a confrontation. Follow
Gandhi. Turn the other cheek.' Ananda had believed his uncle
would weigh in. His mother had told him that his uncle
could argue brilliantly and persuasively when he chose. He
was shocked by this little piece of theatre. He couldn't fathom
the man. Still, he must recoup, gather his wits. He'd turned
his back on him—skulking nuisance and turncoat, skulking
in his macintosh—and opted precisely for confrontation. He
challenged Vishal to a fight. Once he'd issued the challenge,
he was propelled forward by its ballast in that narrow landing.
'Ananda, Ananda!' his mother cried in fear. His own belly was
unsettled by apprehension. 'You want a physical fight?' said

Vishal with perplexity and relish. 'Yeah, a physical fight—and let me warn you that I know karate.' That seemed to calm Vishal at once. He slowed down. 'Hey, why do you want to fight?' he asked. That strategic play was the first small step towards establishing suzerainty over the kitchen. Vishal had moved to new accommodation in two weeks. After about nine months, Ananda's father, visiting from Bombay, prevailed upon Walia to erect that door and cordon the kitchen off and to turn his son's room into a small, self-contained studio. The rent leapt up at once. He was now the flat's sovereign, but had no power over the noises his neighbours made.

* * *

The kitchen was filled with light. Behind him, framed by the window, were the chimneys of other houses. Natural light in the kitchen was bleak; it stood doing nothing, illuminating the fridge, last night's plate and fork under the tap. It was sunlight inside a prison.

He boiled water and made tea. From the carton's spout, whose edges were congealing into a frosty moustache, a splash of milk spilled on to the shelf; he quelled his momentary but frequent irritation with the carton, with mankind, and the dim-witted forces that governed the universe, and wiped the surface with a strip of kitchen tissue. Today he'd make that journey again—on the Northern Line. To his uncle's house. 'House' in a limited sense: it was a bedsit in the basement. But when Ananda thought of the place, it was of the house itself that he thought, 24 Belsize Park, where his uncle had occupied for twenty-one years the first-floor bedsit; then been moved by the Council down below, when a flat in the basement fell vacant and was converted into two bedsits by the Nigerian landlord Ananda had never seen, and repairs begun (in his uncle's former home) on the crumbling ceiling. He'd heard that his uncle's monthly rent—eighteen pounds fifty—was more or less static since 1961; it was possible the landlord wanted the whole first floor back to rent out as a single flat.

He stirred the milk in the mug, till, turning from clear but dark to pale brown and neutrally uniform, the water had become tea-like, the spoon negotiating the vortex it had set in motion by constantly evading, and sometimes colliding into, the submerged leviathan tea bag. Then he'd retrieved it from the pool on to his spoon, at once swollen and unresistant, dead but still smoking, an incredibly ugly thing. Unable to look at it, he tossed it into the bin.

*

His uncle was renowned as a world-conqueror. He'd heard the story time and time again, not least from his uncle. But the story would have no charge, no electricity, if those world-conquering qualities had never been in question. And it was that element of doubt and failure that was, as a result, highlighted in the recountings.

In fact, back home in India, even those who benefited from his uncle's monthly or quarterly handouts, and hadn't seen him in decades, recalled him with a smile in a mildly uncomplimentary way—thinking of the boy, with all his oddities, in Sylhet, and the young man in Shillong, where, just after Independence and Partition, he'd become a used-car salesman despite all his brilliance in school.

By then, 1955, Ananda's father was in London, pursuing without focus his Chartered Accountancy qualifications, while his best friend sold cars in Shillong. Then the friend became his brother-in-law. For Uma travelled across the seas—in an aircraft—and joined Ananda's father Satish (to whom she'd been betrothed before he left Calcutta). This journey—counting the interminable waiting on Uma's part, the six years of not knowing whether or not it would happen, making her a kind of paragon of and authority on waiting—had been so long in the preparation that when it took place other things quickly followed: the wedding on a sunny August day in London, where Uma (or, to everyone, Khuku) was married to Satish in the presence of her younger brother Benoy, who was en route to Germany to train as an engineer. The priest was an exceptionally fair-skinned Punjabi whose Sanskrit sounded intimidatingly convincing and who was in London to study medicine. Most of this Ananda knew several times over (one doesn't go to the epic—Brecht had putatively said—to learn the story, but for the pleasure of hearing it again), from his mother's joyous repetition of the details, and her persistent weaving and shuttling of the mundane loom of memory. The fair-skinned priest, however, was a new element in the tale; he'd only heard about him two months ago.

So hardly any detail in that narrative could surprise Ananda any more, and yet—as was the case two months ago—he was often surprised. The things he hadn't known his mother let slip by accident—for example, the fact that it had been a blazing summer that year in England. He knew, of course, the date of the wedding, and annually, in Bombay, there was an anniversary party when friends came home for dinner—8th August!—'What will you give me on 8th August?'—so she to his father, half-jokingly but with an innocent doggedness a few days prior to the event. And, though Ananda knew that they'd been married in

28

England, he inevitably thought, by default, of 8th August in relationship to Bombay, and only recently did he see and imagine it more clearly—that, for them, the day's history was forever located *here*. Realisation had come a few weeks ago, when his mother was still visiting him. The two of them had left Warren Street behind and were walking past Euston Square, when she pointed to the building of the Hindu Association where they were married, and said, 'Strange, I remember it being much bigger!' Ananda glanced at the landmark. 'Such a bright, dazzling day!' she said. 'And it went on like that after I'd arrived, on and on, the darkness never seeming to come. People told me when I left Shillong, Be prepared for the rain, don't be disheartened by the gloom. That first summer, I had no idea what they meant!'

*

It took her a year, she said to Ananda, to get his father on the rails again. He'd been adrift, distracted after his articleship by politics, poring over M.N. Roy, the 'radical humanist', going to listen to Rajani Palme Dutt speak at the Majlis, having cups of tea with Bengali Marxists, either not writing his exams or casually failing them when he did. She brought him in line. She, a mere matriculate in the third division, who'd never been to college, cast among women who'd either learnt dance and music at Santiniketan or were from Calcutta—she saw her husband's future lay in her hands. And so her arrival into

29

London was primarily to salvage and rescue. Ananda knew well she had these capacities. His mother, with whom he only quarrelled as a child, resenting her disciplinarian rages, her angry, too-large, flashing eyes, he'd begun to see—since he was sixteen—carried irreducible strength. At five foot one and a half inches, at once a diminutive, round-nosed busybody and the closest he'd known to the goddesses of myth. Wasn't he, in his recent doting upon her, being fanciful? Of course he was—he knew that.

*

Even when she'd arrived here in 1955, unable to speak perfect English, noticeably little, it became clear she was a force and that she could command respect—maybe even intimidate. Implausibly, she got a job at the Naval Advisory Department in the Indian High Commission at Aldwych. At the interview, she made it a point to answer the questions her husband had coached her to expect, though those questions weren't asked. She settled into employment, which involved an irregular sending out of memos to and receiving them from various commanders of the Indian navy. The High Commission had been seized by a 'reorganisation', and the result was that, in six months, at the end of the reorganisation—a word whose significance she grasped slightly, but whose melee she was happy to be part of—she was drawing a handsome salary of fifty-eight pounds a month, enough to look after Satish's

30

needs and hers, and give him time to devote himself entirely to the shrine of accountancy.

She sat at her desk in India House, comfortably negligent of office friendships, openly disdainful of the gossip between the Indian women near her, Mrs Sinha and Mrs Hussein, forensically perplexed by the conversations Englishwomen had ('So she said . . . and I said . . . and then she said . . .'). She mimicked and relived these 'He said' and 'She said' for her husband. Going to the cinema, they agreed that the English, unlike the melodramatic Indians, were natural actors; but they also noted that this race behaved and spoke in normal circumstances like they were in a film, with a peculiar self-consciousness, as if their gestures and words were being recorded. There didn't appear to be a complete separation between fantasy and social life for the English. Dr Krishnan, the departmental head, had discovered what an exceptional singer she was, and was willing to overlook her eccentric uninvolvement in office life. 'She is an artist, and she is an asset,' he said, meaning it was okay for her to not fit in. He encouraged her to sing at the India Office's public functions—on numerous commemorations and national days. Not everyone liked this. Miss Watkins, her immediate superior, resented her privileges and chafed at her. Then, one morning, when she'd commanded her: 'Uma, bring me that file!', Khuku had lost her calm—as she did periodically—and tossed it towards Miss Watkins's table, saying, '*There's* your file!' (Ananda, hearing this episode recounted, thought how

31

his mother loved to throw things when she was angry. The servants knew it. Her husband knew it.) This was followed by an instant of scandalised undecidedness. Yet Miss Watkins didn't retaliate. In the next few months, she was unflinchingly civil to Khuku. When Dr Krishnan died suddenly of a heart attack, Khuku was transferred to the consular department on South Audley Street.

Khuku's propensity to battle was innate to her. Besides possessing an inexplicable tendency to be joyous—she could never be sad or angry for long—she'd had an inexplicable conviction from childhood that she was destined for great contentment. She'd never believed she'd live forever either in Sylhet or Shillong; and, with or without the transfer, neither Aldwych nor South Audley Street could hold her. This was part of the hope she conveyed to Ananda: that nothing, including Warren Street, was long-term. Her readiness for battle she had even today. When trouble presented itself, she had to confront it with her oppositional littleness.

When the Patels had moved into the rooms upstairs, Ananda's mother was visiting, and staying with him in the studio flat. After two or three nights, it dawned on them that the Patels would be noisy. Noise invaded the flat from different directions—from below (Mandy's radio) and above. Ananda began to obsess over the Patels' movements. At 11.30 p.m., he found his mother had slipped out irresistibly—it was more in response to his anxiety than to the noise that she'd done this—and gone up the flight of stairs. He followed her in sheepish excitement, remonstrating 'Ma! Ma!', unable to pull her back, till they were in the attic's half-lit converted kitchen, a den in which Vivek Patel and Cynthia and Cynthia's brother Rahul and Shashank were pouring wine into glasses, talking, laughing loudly. Khuku had ambushed them; they were taken by surprise. Though Vivek attempted to refute her in his labile, lisping way, and Cynthia giggled, and Rahul, most disconcertingly of the four, exuded a silent, myopic rage, his mother stood in the eye of Walia's converted kitchen and lectured them. Her message, implicitly—but also forthright, without prevarication—was that her son was doing a 'real' degree (unlike them) at a 'real' university, he'd embarked on a difficult voyage, his father was paying through his nose, and she—the timeless Indian mother that she was (and more)— would brook no partying as the hour approached midnight. They defiantly invoked the equivalent of their constitutional rights, but in the end they let her be, as if she was mad. Maybe the Patels had become a bit more self-aware about their stomping; only they couldn't *help* making a racket.

*

She had gone. Eight days ago. Ascended swiftly into the air. Like a bird. Taken that proud national aircraft Air India: nodded to the Maharajah. She was back home with his father.

* * *

Unwashed, evacuated, clothed in the night's kurta and pyjamas, he sat on the rug to sing. He was an exile in his home. He frequently expected complaints. He knew the ragas he sang were hopelessly alien to Mandy's ear (she too slept till midday) and foreign even to the boys upstairs. Not one of them (certainly not Ananda) ever saw the sun rise; though maybe the Patels sometimes went to bed when it was just coming up. Now Ananda made a clarion call to the day with the raga Bhairav (though it was already nine thirty). He hardly let a morning pass without practising—he was a singer in his own solitude, he was his own audience and his notes needed to sound perfect to himself. Without practising his voice would falter. He sat cross-legged on the rug—all rugs in London houses were the same—with the tanpura on his lap: it was no bigger than a ukelele, made by a septuagenarian, Ambalal Sitari. The old man received visitors in a room in Breach Candy—Ananda's music teacher had taken him there and cajoled the old man to part with the portable tanpura: 'He will be in London soon, and he is dedicated: he practises every day—in fact, I have to tell him not to practise so much!' The strings didn't speak; they had a flat sound, however much Ananda manipulated the threads at the lower end—the tanpura wouldn't drone, and was barely audible even in the studio flat's deep quiet, but he kept worrying it, nestling the instrument. Ambalal Sitari's experiment hadn't come off. The wood, which should have become a living thing, remained, stubbornly, wood; the strings were muted.

*

He sang: he'd trained himself to be thick-skinned. It was a quarter to ten—it was *their* problem if they went to bed late, then slept slothfully into the hours when people were at work. They *couldn't* expect midnight-stillness at this time. He sang delicately; singing was his mode, in his student's life of subterfuge and anonymity (he hardly ever went to lectures and only a handful of professors knew him), of being battle-ready, in constant preparedness. It was a battle—this struggle to master Bhairav—almost without a cause or end. Twenty minutes into the exposition, there was a stirring above. The movement of a beast: a first random thump then silence, then—making Ananda uneasy—another thump. It was the alienness of the melody that intruded on their drunken sleep. 'Karma Chameleon' would have just lulled them, late in the morning, to sounder sleep.

* * *

No, Mandy was definitely up. She'd just cleared her throat; a female throat-clearing, melodious—but threatening. He and Mandy had a sort of duet going—of noises, of complaints. The first time was soon after he'd moved into the flat; term had begun, his parents were still staying with him before they flew back. It was early October, warm, and the window was three or four inches open, allowing in footfall, snatches of song, a shout from near the tube. Then there was an intrusion of another kind, of atmospheric noise as he lay back, head on the plump pillow. A hubbub with a wash of background music, as if he were, without warning, in the centre of a metropolis, roaming in the town square. He must have dreamed this, sound and image mixing with one another as he dozed off. But no, on second thought, he was awake and conscious of floating above the crowded hubbub. Ah, a party! In the flat downstairs! He couldn't believe he was privy to this bonhomie. He asked his mother, unconvinced he wasn't dreaming: 'Can you hear it?'

After midnight, not bothering to change out of his pyjamas, he went down, knocked on Mandy's door, and—sensing fleetingly the figures in the background—told her he couldn't sleep.

*

Mandy was in her twenties. Sometimes she looked older; as if she might be in her early thirties. She kept uncertain hours. She'd come home at three in the morning, shut the door with a bang, turn on cheery music. She told him that she did her aerobic exercises at that hour. She'd shared this information when he'd pointed out to her indignantly: 'Mandy—what about you?—must you, must you play that music at half past three or four in the morning?' His question was meant to counter hers: 'Must you sing in the morning? It drives me crazy! It's like Chinese torture.' 'I *have* to practise at half past nine,' he'd said. 'Besides, it's well after the day has begun.' 'I know, but I come home very late—I work at a bar twice a week.' 'I'm sorry, Mandy,' he'd said, attempting to shrug. 'I do have to practise.' On some days, she worked as a temp— probably a receptionist. She went out in the morning with the music playing all day—low, but continual, inoffensive, except that it was bubblegum pop. He queried her about why it was necessary for the music to play in an empty flat, and she told him it wasn't empty; the music was for her budgies, so they wouldn't be frightened or alone.

Ananda had never seen or heard her budgies; it was the first he'd become aware of the birds. He'd never seen the inside of her flat except once, when she'd knocked on his door and nonchalantly asked him to help her change a light bulb. There was an erotic charge running beneath the way they chafed and got on each other's nerves—or was he imagining it? It had seemed, as she spectated upon him climbing a chair and reaching for the ceiling (again, in his pyjamas), that she was capable of dealing with the light bulb herself. But he was very proper and a little cowardly too—he barely glanced at

37

She'd had her revenge for their constant tit for tat once the payphone incident occurred—that night when the Patels and Cynthia's incongruously studious-looking brother Rahul had dislodged the BT coin box from the landing between the first and second floors and taken it to the attic, breathing heavily with exertion and laughter. Ananda had heard it all—it must have been past 1 a.m.—the rushed activity, the transitory out-of-place jingling; but he didn't know what to think of it. Next morning, he saw the discoloured blank space where the coin box was. Walia arrived, hovered around Mandy's door, and questioned her about what happened. Ananda, dully listening from upstairs, heard her say: 'I think it was Ananda.' He was overcome: less disturbed than wounded—and, most importantly, made intensely and doubly to feel a foreigner. Every fibre of his being said, 'What am I doing here? This is not my home,' though no words formed in his head. He heard Walia dismiss the accusation in a bland matter-of-fact way: 'No, no, it wouldn't be *him*, it must be the boys upstairs.' And Ananda felt the sense of vindication that only an eavesdropper and exile might feel, that a man he hardly knew, Walia, should still know him well enough to have made up his mind about him. When he related this conversation to his uncle later, he saw him pass, in a wave, through the same emotions, from disbelief to shock to a kind of scandalised but grateful relief. 'Well, at least he has enough up there to know you'd never do something like that,' he muttered. Ananda was surprised that his uncle had someone to a summer's day—except to insult the addressee? A near-imbecilic line.

Shall I compare thee to a summer's day?

But, no; it was beautiful. He'd reread the sonnet, for his preparations for the Renaissance paper, and then, after reacting against it through its earlier associations, read it once again, allowing himself to understand it. The lines had begun to repeat themselves in his head, like a jingle in a commercial. The poet—what was he up to? He'd meant to extol his beloved—not by saying she was as good as a summer's day, but better! Letting the wooden frame nestle his chin, Ananda daydreamed, studying Tandoor Mahal and its curtains.

Thou art more lovely and more temperate.

More lovely, *more* temperate! So the poet was dissing the summer's day, then, in order to praise his beloved. Yet what apposite terms for this summer, as a season, or in its incarnation as a single day: 'lovely', with its suggestion of innocence and newborn qualities; 'temperate', indicating calm, modesty, and fortuitously echoing 'temporal', with its hint of the short-lived. 'Lovely' carried in it the sense of the short-lived too; the loveliness of 'lovely' was contingent on it not being eternal. And so the summer's day was transient in comparison to the poet's beloved, who'd continue to prosper

41

and grow to 'eternal lines' in the effing sonnet. To emphasise this, Shakespeare must diss the English spring and summer in the third and fourth lines again:

Rough winds do shake the darling buds of May,
And summer's lease hath all too short a date.

It was the fragility and the undependability of the English summer that Shakespeare was drawing the reader's attention to—hoping, thereby, that the contrast would aggrandise his lover's qualities. But, for Ananda, it was summer—by being contingent—that came to brief life on his rediscovery of the poem in London, and not the beloved, immobile and fixed in eternity; because the imagination is drawn—not by sympathy, but some perverse definition of delight—to the fragile, the animated, and the short-lived. In this unlikely manner, the near-imbecilic sonnet had been returning to him in the last four days.

* * *

A butterfly had settled on the upper window. It had closed its wings, simulating a leaf, or engendering a geometric angle, perfect as a shadow, but was now wavering and bending to one side—not out of any obedience to the breeze, but according to a whim. Almost nothing—but for this pane with faint blotches of mildew—separated it in its world outside (Warren Street) from the studio flat within, from where Ananda measured it, intrigued. All insects made him apprehensive. Where had this rarity come from? The principal danger of summer, he'd found, were bees. Almost every day one came in without invitation. He had to pretend he was unmoved by its floating, persistent exploration of the room, until, unable to cohabit with it an instant longer, his nerves already on edge, he'd have to, with an almost superhuman effort, quickly push the window up halfway, causing the house to tremble to its foundations, and then rally to chase it out with something appropriate—usually a copy of the *Times* or the *Times Literary Supplement*. The comedy and even the undeniable magic of that chase became clear to him the moment the bee had escaped, the room was empty but for him, and—like someone in a storm—he grappled with lowering the window again.

He saw now, suddenly, that the butterfly was gone—the street's voyager; undertaking short, unsteady bursts of flight past Walia's flats.

* * *

2

Telemachus and Nestor
(and Manny-loss)

Stupidly, he'd set up a meeting with Nestor Davidson for midday. Some resistant part of him would rather have lolled about—masturbating occasionally, perhaps, though his penis was sore; or dipping into the *Oxford Companion to Modern British Literature*, to spy, once more, on cherished lines and phrases (most of them these days by Edward Thomas), to check if they still existed and possessed the same shock of surprise; or watching, agog, children's TV—*Postman Pat*, whose English village of workaday encounters and visits was so much more preferable to the turbulent life of Noddy that Ananda had come to know as a child; then there was the man he's begun to like even better—Mr Benn.

These children's stories were where craft and observation lay; qualities abnegated by the grown-up shows. Ananda loved the way Postman Pat's van appeared, like a private revelation, muffled yet exact, a speck of red on the hill, moving, disappearing, until it appeared again, closer this time. He was oddly touched by this trickery, the vanishing and reappearance. Mr Benn vanished too. A cheery man in a black suit and bowler hat, who, each day, escaped life's tedium by going into a tailor's shop and slipping into another universe through a mirror in the fitting room. Ananda envied the enclosedness of that fitting room. Where better to lose yourself? There was a naivety and melancholy about Mr Benn that struck a chord with Ananda, but also reminded him of the sort of unmoored bachelor whom he, despite himself, was drawn to—his uncle, for example. The animation was rudimentary, and, instead of Mr Benn talking, you had a remarkably reassuring, paternal voice-over—that spoke only to *you*. Paucity of means and of technology—*that* was it; that was what brought to these programmes their peculiar but unmissable artistry. Ananda saw that. Art was not only about not saying everything; it was about not being *able* to say everything. Thus Chaplin's films—dependent as they were on dance and choreography—were superior to so many instances of the talkies, including Chaplin's own work, given the talkies had the dubious advantage of speech and storytelling. As things became easier to tell, they became plainer, more transparent, boring even. Art was synonymous with impediment.

* * *

But no Mr Benn today! He must see Mr Davidson instead.
(He couldn't persuade himself to call him 'Nestor'—though
all students addressed their teachers by their first names—not
just because of the oddity of the name, but his prissy sense of
formality, his Hindu—he was no practising Hindu—distaste
of contact: the Mr and Ms So and So he used was not only
a mode of deference, but a mawkish reassurance: 'I won't be
presumptuous. We'll keep our distance.') It had to be Mr
because Nestor Davidson was neither Dr—he had a BA from
London University—nor Professor: he was, in fact, a Reader.
So the Mr, democratic, anonymous, and somehow, in its two
humdrum syllables, quintessentially English, had to suffice.
It would do.

*

His first two years—at university and out of it—had
been painful. Firstly, there was the civilisation itself, with
its language—a language only secondarily his—its zebra
crossings, where cars slowed down and waited, pulsating,
its assortment of tea bags and cheese and pickle sandwiches,
its dry, clipped way of speaking. He felt terribly excluded.
Or chose to be excluded; it gave his drift and insignificance
meaning in his own eyes. The students in the college—they
filled him with nervousness and distrust because of their pink
complexions and blue eyes, their easy taking for granted of
each other: an American accent, overheard, for some reason

brought him momentary lightness. In this way, he'd curtailed his visits to the college till, by the middle of the first year, he wasn't attending a single lecture. He only appeared for his tutorials. During one of these, his tutor, a beautiful young woman called Hilary Burton, broached the subject of his meagre interface with college life: 'Mrs Bailey, the Anglo-Saxon tutor, says you've stopped going to her seminar.' It was the first sign that his irregularities—the liberties he'd taken in a smooth, self-governing institution that had no knowledge of him—had been noted. 'I told her you haven't been well; that you've been getting migraines,' said Dr Burton, appraising his collar, eyes downcast, neutral but sympathetic. 'I know what they're like'—lowering her soft voice to a minuscule register—'I get them too.' He was vulnerable to headaches (he must have mentioned this to her some time) as he was plagued by hyperacidity. The two could be linked in an ecological chain. Migraines arose from, among other things, lack of sleep; hyperacidity on some nights destroyed rest; and Migraleve—which he kept at only a marginally less accessible spot than Double Action Rennie—could, if he wasn't mindful, create hyperacidity. At least a few of his ailments were siblings, and now and then they chose to unite against him. Still, the consequence of Dr Burton's words—a complaint relayed, but shared like a confidence—was that Ananda went to the remaining four of Mrs Bailey's seminars, before giving up on Anglo-Saxon when it became a non-compulsory option in the second year. And so he was introduced to this primitive tongue, which had letters—like the malformed p—that had no equivalent or peer in modern English, a tongue used by proselytisers and, after the Norman Conquest, by servants. It had a claustrophobic air—not just of an island-language, but of a further retreat from the world. How remote it was from the worldly, aerated domains of Sanskrit, Persian, and Greek! It was hidden. Yet there was more to it than translated passages from the Bible (one or the other of the parables of the New Testament that were the seminar's staple) which concluded inevitably with a gruff threat: that those who didn't adhere to God's ways would be 'cast into the outer darkness with much gnashing of teeth'. No, there was more to the study of Anglo-Saxon than this scary outer darkness and the dull acoustics of teeth-gnashing: such as 'The Dream of the Rood', with its flaring cross, burning through time, and its warrior-Christ, more a hero than a blonde prophet. Poring over these texts gave to Ananda his first inkling that medieval England was different from what he'd glimpsed of it in movies: that the Christians here used to be stranger than any conjecture of them suggested. And, despite it being so long, the language ugly and resistant, the words heaped like debris, he was gripped by 'The Battle of Maldon', and even asked Mrs Bailey, 'Is Byrhtnoth, then, a Christian martyr or tragic hero?'—a mouthful, that name—and the pretty girl whose name he still didn't know (he was so deprived of sex—disabled through shyness and race-consciousness—so lonely!) glanced up at him with a flicker of curiosity, and Mrs trying to hide her exasperation, brandishing his essay, said: 'You write very eloquently, Mr Sen'—it took three meetings for her to graduate coquettishly to his first name; she'd even asked whether she was pronouncing the simple monosyllabic surname accurately—'and what I like is that—unlike my other students—you've taken the poem for what it fundamentally *is*: a *love* story!' How could he not? He was a passionate apologist for love. He was like a virginal Victorian girl: love and sex existed in separate compartments. He would argue and argue that year and the next for love in the jaded circles of the English department—the Vision of Eros, which, as Auden had said, was near-impossible to champion. For to speak of love was like 'talking about ghosts'—'most people had heard of them, but very few people knew one'. He sensed that Hilary Burton's encouragement was a backhanded compliment. A connoisseur of literary insincerity, she herself was being completely insincere: and wanted him to know it. Last time, she'd suggested that *Troilus and Criseyde* was not so much a poem as a forerunner of the novel, exemplifying not the poem's 'truth' but the novel's 'light and shade'. This observation was symptomatic of a general call to arms within the department, and he first became aware of it in Dr Burton's room; that the student needed to be educated about how the idea that literature was a repository of emotion and spontaneity was only a relatively recent Romantic fiction, no more than two centuries old, that most students had been schooled, without being aware of it, in this Romantic withdrawn completely into late-night television shows, radio talks, and journal-publishing. If only Spender had frequented these corridors now, Ananda wouldn't have been so unhappy. It was not so much his poems Ananda cared about—although he loved Hughes's and Larkin's work, Spender's poetry hadn't made an impression—as the appearance (slightly stooped; tweed-jacketed; with a blue-eyed angelic face, like David Gower's) and the persona he'd encountered in *World within World*: sensitive, with a youth of mildly adventurous left-wing predilections, but a firm believer in poetry's sacrosanct qualities ('I think continually of those who are great'). If only Spender had survived in the college to Ananda's arrival, he would have recognised in him a kindred soul, a person moved invisibly by the poetic. Ananda would have hesitantly shown his poems to Spender, who, in his excitement, would have got them published, just as Spender's friend Auden had once tremblingly, in astonishment, discovered the nineteen-year-old Dom Moraes's poetry on a visit to Bombay, and been instrumental in its publication. That collection, as everyone knew, was the one book by an Indian to win the Hawthornden Prize, its author the youngest to have received that accolade. If Ananda had won the Hawthornden, he wouldn't have been as young as Moraes, but young enough. Instead, he'd come to the college just a little too late. He recalled that Spender, in his memoir, had mentioned a teacher in his school, St Paul's, who'd said to him, 'You're unhappy in school, but you are going to be very happy at university.' Ananda had almost taken route he didn't intend to take? Brightest students! Was she inveigling him with disingenuous noises? By this time, her health—which had been appalling beneath her beautiful exterior and her gay fauvist dresses—had worsened, and she couldn't see properly; so that when she stared at his collar while speaking, it was neither shyness nor flirtatiousness which made her do so, but simply the fact that she had a hazy sense now of where his face was. She'd been diagnosed with a problem in the brain—he had no idea what it was—a year ago. He wasn't sure how much of the illness was real, how much a product of her imagination.

Medieval England didn't attract him; not Gawain, not *Piers Plowman*. He felt he'd like Greek tragedy, but kept putting off the 'intellectual background' classes where he could familiarise himself with Aeschylus and Sophocles. Besides, he was becoming suspicious of tragedy. He put this down to the rediscovery of his Indian past, his recent realisation that there was no tragedy in Sanskrit literature. Sanskrit theatre, with its tranquil curtain calls, where thief, courtesan, soldier, king, could smilingly take a bow, their conflicts resolved—*that* was a welcome antidote to the Western universe, with its privileging of dark over light. He was a proponent of joy! This, despite being drawn to Philip Larkin. He was plainly prejudiced against the West. Then what was he doing *in* the West, in the English department? He was clearly not at home; he was lost. He'd always presumed that Sophocles rhymed with 'monocles'. Until, standing before a noticeboard announcing lectures, his mispronunciation was gently overlooked by a fellow student, an English boy, who repeated the name, rhyming it with Pericles. Ananda was embarrassed.

What of the epics, which they made such a fuss over? He'd gone to a lecture on the *Aeneid* one Monday morning, and puzzled over the lecturer's caressing pronunciation—*e-nee-yud*; but he—the lecturer—had droned on about the 'founding myth of the nation', and Ananda, in the back row, began to turn the pages of the *Observer* stealthily (two students glanced at him, smiling). What to make of these epics in comparison to the Ramayana and the Mahabharata, the latter (he was now convinced) equal to all of Shakespeare and more?—they were like a Thames to the Ganges, a stream beside a river with no noticeable horizon; minor. Homer he'd studied with similar scepticism, noting that the 'rosy-fingered dawn' recurred without volition, like a traffic light, every few pages of the *Iliad*, and, with greater fascination—salivating, even, because he was often hungry—how the soldiers feasted on pork 'singed in its own fat' at regular intervals. The *Odyssey* he hadn't bothered to read.

Still, he'd read enough of and around the Greeks to know that the gods were undependable, and put their powers to use in idiosyncratic ways. In this, they were superficially like the many-headed, many-armed Hindu deities; except that, with the Hindu gods, you felt the capriciousness of their actions was linked to the transformative play of creation, *lila*. In comparison, the Greek gods were merely dim-witted and vengeful. They hibernated; they woke up; they became conscious of a problem; they either attended to it or forgot to. There was no telling which human being they'd help out or do their utmost to destroy—guided by some personal like or grudge that had no rational explanation, or, what was quite common, in order to redress a slight received aeons ago.

* * *

Ananda first met Dr Burton on Gower Street. She was wearing a bright orange dress with large yellow circles which came to below her knees, and was tapping the pavement with a cane. He knew it was her. It was the first time that the person he wanted someone to be turned out to be whom he thought it was. 'Mr Sen!' she exclaimed, taking particular pleasure in the sound of his voice, as if it were a disembodied stream. 'We have a meeting at ten, don't we?' It was drizzling very lightly, despite the sun, and instinctively, opportunely, he took her under his umbrella. 'Can you help me?' she asked. 'I have a problem with my vision today.' He placed his arm on her shoulder, not daring to keep it there for more than a few seconds at a time, but feeling an unbelievable closeness that she too seemed to have surrendered to, almost patting her back as he steered her forward. From Gower Street they entered through a heavy glass door on the left and were in a long bleak corridor, from where—he escorting her, but she guiding him, as she knew the way—they ended up (he couldn't remember how) in another building, and at last in her spacious room on the first floor, where the medievalists, Chaucerians, and linguistics professors had their offices.

Their romance remained buried beneath their different personalities; his still unformed, but with many of its traits already visible. She never found out if he had a sense of humour; and he could only deduce she had one from the poster on her door, showing a languorous Mrs Thatcher being carried masterfully by Ronald Reagan in his arms.

Her kindness, like her cane, he knew only from her curious exhibitions of empathy, such as the birdhouse she kept on her sill for transient but recurrent sparrows. He couldn't crack, through her, what Englishness was; and, for her, the prickly mystery of being Indian clearly remained permanently unsolved. Sex stayed in the air, like an absurdity; once, when he asked her if he could write a tutorial essay on a topic different from what she'd suggested, she'd parted her legs, both swift and interminably slow—she was in a shortish skirt, he'd had to turn his eyes away—before crossing them again, and said, smiling faintly, 'Do what you like. I believe in the pleasure principle.' He was unhappy about her tutelage—he was generally unhappy at the time—but masturbated thinking about her, twice.

In the second academic year (which had ended a month ago), he no longer saw her—which was a relief. He wanted to forget her, at least for now. She had taken ill; his second-year tutor told him one day that her visits had grown irregular. How had the subject come up—of Hilary Burton? Maybe from a recounting to the second-year tutor of his state of mind in the first year. Another day, the tutor announced—again, an association of anecdotes and harmless gossip led unexpectedly to her—that Dr Burton had entered a coma. She was alive. Her brain wasn't. She was too young. Ananda couldn't believe it.

* * *

His second-year tutor, Richard Bertram, he was happier with. By some train of thought, Richard—maybe his surname— made Ananda think of P.G. Wodehouse, and this at once put him at ease. Richard, with his general cheeriness, and his mild astonishment each time Ananda came for a tutorial—'Hel-*lo* there Ananda!'—didn't belie this impression. He was very tall, which added to his air of being a large schoolboy who was destined to thrive in an educational institution. You could see him sometimes in the corridor, negotiating his bicycle by the handle, his trousers fastened with bicycle clips round his ankles, urgent and unselfconscious, confirming he had no natural habitat but college.

*

He was kind to Ananda, but was of a different species altogether—a Renaissance scholar. Like Hilary Burton, he was a product of Oxford, and this meant he was like one who'd assiduously made his way back to reality from a dream. The fact that the Renaissance was Richard's intellectual domain meant there was—despite their bonhomie—an unspoken gulf between tutor and student, which was palpable to Ananda alone, and of which Richard was blissfully unmindful. Ananda viewed Richard with gratitude and friendship, but also anthropologically: as an English academic of a particular ilk and type. The reason was this—Ananda couldn't seriously engage (whatever pretence he made) with someone whose interests were anterior to 1800. The nineteenth century was a subconscious cut-off date; behind it lay an incredible array of armadas, knaves, kings, people on horseback; Philip Sydney's *Arcadia* and Spenser's *Faerie Queene*. Even in the nineteenth century, it was only Wordsworth, Coleridge, Blake, and select bits of Shelley and Keats that he felt a loyalty towards, for their wonder at the actual universe; the deliberately histrionic (Byron and Browning) he avoided, even if he was intermittently susceptible to their gifts; the Victorians, too, whatever their persuasion—Tennyson, Clough, Housman— he'd cross the street in order not to have to meet them. Richard didn't suspect at all how prone to irrational literary biases Ananda was: he was too self-absorbed and congenitally trustful to be suspicious. For Ananda—though he may not have articulated it to himself plainly, and despite its horrible wars and conflicts (and maybe not entirely unconnected to them)—the twentieth century was the most magnificent period ever. At once tragic and playful, so incredible and unparalleled, yet so familiar that you might not notice it! It was either taken for granted, because it was merely the present, or praised for the wrong reasons, because it represented progress; it was easy not to really think about it. Did Richard think of it—since, after all, he was of it, and in it? Twentieth-century literature! With its narrow subject, modern man—strange creature! With his retinue of habits, like getting on to buses, known novelist—but not well-known enough for Ananda to have heard of him before he came to this college. Ananda was apprehensive when Davidson was assigned as his temporary tutor—the set mouth, the determined look, the nose, made him wonder about his temper.

In fact, it became evident very early that Mr Davidson and Ananda found the same kinds of thing funny. Mr Davidson (unlike Ananda's first two tutors) was not shy of calling people 'idiots', and their laughter at randomly chosen human beings was essential to their common enjoyment of life as they sat down to tutorials. Midway through the tutorial, they broke to have tea, and biscuits from a large oval tin. Mr Davidson didn't consume that much alcohol, so the nose had no explanation. On the shelves on the left—on which the sun fell directly—were books by Isherwood, Fitzgerald (*Tender Is the Night*), Babel, Pound, Auden, Eliot, Bruno Schulz, Emily Dickinson, D.H. Lawrence, Singer, Olive Schreiner, and what were presumably his novels, *An Outing in the Summer*, *Boer Diamonds*, *Intransigents*, with his very own name (yes, that's what it was)—Ananda glanced at it twice without giving himself away—descending the spine. Any place where you have a collection of books must be considered a second home, and when a man unobtrusively collects books he once wrote it hints at the fact he's maybe not inwardly settled. Mr Davidson was from South Africa; this accounted for the accent, which had had Ananda puzzling privately. He had come to London in the early sixties. Here he'd met the woman he only ever called 'Sal', and to whom he was married. In the college library, Ananda had stealthily read the first chapter of Nestor Davidson's memoir, *Time Regained*, and, in the silence that he seldom entered or visited (he'd only been to the library one other time), he was struck by the vividness with which the arrival was described, the first encounter with King's Cross Station, a journey made with a friend to look for digs at Highgate, the discovery as a bewildered loiterer of the backstreets of Victoria. Could one hold even London in wonder and affection? He himself was so at odds with London. As he held the book before him, he thought in a flash of his parents, who also spoke of their first bleak years in this crushing city with a kind of love.

*

Nestor Davidson was Jewish: a man fitting in, seamlessly, without any special attempt to do so, but having to fit in nevertheless. Was this what had made Ananda's and his paths converge—the fact there was room here for them both, Mr Davidson with his Lithuanian forefathers of whom he knew relatively little, Ananda with his covert Sylheti ancestry? No, that was too fanciful. Maybe it was simply that they both loved 'modern' literature. After meeting Mr Davidson, Ananda, for the first time, had felt there was a point to his being here; that he was moving in the right direction after all.

* * *

The right direction! But he was late. It was 11.35, it would take him twenty minutes to reach Mr Davidson's door. That is, if he picked up momentum and didn't dawdle on Tottenham Court Road. For his journeys in the neighbourhood hardly ever had a purpose. Today was an exception—but even this was more of an unofficial meeting between a mature writer and an apprentice than a tutorial: term was over, his second academic year was history. He sat on the bed, tied his laces, got up. Alone. No mother to see him off, no stream of meaningless mother-chatter to soften his exit. It was quiet with her not there. One part of him still listened, alert, for the Patels. Nothing. He closed the door behind him, went down the tunnel of stairs, the jaundice-yellow rug lit evenly by yellow light, swinging quickly at the first landing to avert the possibility of an emerging Mandy—more than her intolerance of his singing it was her betrayal that had shaken him—and then, alighting from the last flight of stairs, he was in the ground-floor hallway, the floor covered indiscriminately with the glossy detritus of this morning's junk mail—somehow attesting to the fact that much of the day had already elapsed while the thicker letters in white or brown envelopes—final reminders to pay gas bills; missives from the home office—lay bunched by an invisible hand, piled neatly, on the central heating radiator on the side. Ananda paused to peer at them before deciding that this mix of the daily precipitation of official communications and a suspiciously non-committal package addressed to Vivek Patel, probably containing a pornographic magazine, had nothing for him. He opened the door and, once he'd passed the little vestibule—where often garbage bags were kept—turned right towards McDonald's.

*

Here, at McDonald's—whose burgers were both disappointing and too expensive for him, the big Mac, for its size, a Herculean task to bite into, but strangely nondescript to the palate—was a junction at which you encountered people crossing from Tottenham Court Road into the futuristic anonymity of Euston Road. Others headed through the glass door for (or emerged heavy with) a Big Mac meal, and still others, across the road, milled before Warren Street tube station, either about to disappear inwards, or just coming out, accustoming themselves to the right angle of Warren Street and Tottenham Court Road.

Ananda turned right into the wide busy stretch that went much further than the brain could accommodate; for he had trouble comprehending that *this* Tottenham Court Road was identical to the one after the traffic lights that would sever New Oxford from Oxford Street—*there* lay the more salacious stretch, besides of course the obscure guitar shops in by-lanes, and Foyles, civilised sentinel; but also prostitutes so down-at-heel that you flinched and looked away—they becoming, for a split second, focussed on you as you passed by, giving you the privilege of their attention (it was nice to be noticed, however you might deny it, when you were in the crowd), but becoming bored instantaneously and returning to their vigil; in further by-lanes were the remaining XXX cinemas that, under Thatcher, had become pristine with nipples and buttocks and never the vestige of an erection, the LIVE PEEP SHOW! signs, bursting with unfounded optimism, and the weirder notices pinned to doors: MODELS ON THE FIRST FLOOR. In his first year, he'd been a flâneur of these sites, a frequenter of interiors in which no one acknowledged anyone else as they browsed in stops and starts, and even the faint touch of another man's shoulder could make you flinch, shops that you slipped into through curtains that had been passed through a shredder; he was uneasy, but the shop assistant (if you could call them that: they were probably on parole) was usually friendly, but sly; only once or twice had Ananda received a whiff of racism, a burly man saying 'Vindaloo, vindaloo' in an eerie sing-song to himself. Such people were to be ignored and avoided; there are certain demoniacal beings in the universe, his uncle had said, quoting Taranath the tantric, who are dim but incredibly powerful; they can grow a hundred times their size in a second; they have brute strength; they can fly; but they are not intelligent. You won't be able to beat them in a contest of strength, but you have to hold your nerve when facing them. His uncle's reason for

Lal Qila. He felt no remorse—his uncle was a well-to-do man (though he might have lost his job), without a family or property to his name. Surely he could take them out once a week? So ran the unwritten rule (unchallenged, to date, by his uncle).

*

He turned left at Heal's. When he'd first moved to Warren Street—still fresh to this terrain—he'd taken the longer route, crossing the road at McDonald's and, quite alone—there were hardly any pedestrians here—traversed a no-man's land, passing, each day, a largely unvisited sari emporium, aware that Drummond Street and the Asian grocers and bhelpuri shops weren't far; walked, walked, in silence, till he reached Euston Square tube station. Here, as he turned sharply right facing the station, the vista of Gower Street and his destiny— of being condemned to being in London, of making this journey to college—presented themselves plainly. The grey buildings on his left were the college's, and, midway through the walk, you passed the old grand building and entrance— faux renaissance with its white dome, marked by imperial pretensions, befitting of Rome rather than the surrounding London brick and stone. This entrance was out of bounds; the grand building was being salvaged and renovated from before he'd seen it almost two years ago; it was an irrelevance;

he simply walked past it, noting its brief dishevelment, before he reached the traffic lights, and turned left. It took him two weeks to realise that he needn't take that walk, that he could go down Tottenham Court Road till he reached the Goodge Street underground, and turn into the street bordered by Heal's. This was a better route, less stark and nineteenth-century, less emblematic of the colonial past—what a poor subject he'd have made, even worse than the maladroit he was as a migrant student!—and more consolingly drab and populous. The scattered signs of old and new wealth flanked him on this trip; Heal's, with its fluttering pennants, was a palace, and he had no reason, now or in the future, to enter it to survey the heavy furniture displayed within. Habitat was next to it, with its perky designs, its transformed shapes and fragile-looking chairs and tables; he and his mother, small and bright in her sari, had roamed here one afternoon, and she'd bought him the dining table—it was on a thirty per cent reduction—that now took up one tenth of his room. Much more sprightly, this route. Gower Street—Tagore! What *had* Tagore felt about Gower Street? Ananda had heard that Tagore had enrolled in the same college in 1879 to read Law. He'd attended a few lectures—but not on Law, as far as he knew, but by Herbert Spencer. To be anonymous, a nobody, *and* a subject! This, no doubt, was what had made Ananda shiver slightly when going down Gower Street: the haunting of Empire. Tagore had fled back home, long before taking a degree, in disgrace. Ananda would have fled, too, if he'd come here in 1879; he could barely bring himself to continue in Thatcher's multiracial capital. His mother's visits—her company, the constant chatter in the room—had kept him from returning; poor Tagore had had no rescuing angel, no mother-love to protect and entertain him. Nor, for that matter, had he had Ananda's uncle. Though his uncle couldn't be trusted. Not only was he seldom sympathetic towards Ananda's outpourings of homesickness, he claimed he never felt homesick himself. He was lying.

* * *

Mr Davidson too, surely, had unwittingly persuaded him against going back. He'd calmed him, praised the essays—not polite praise, but kindly recognition—making Ananda think he could maybe persevere.

Down the industrial path Ananda went, past the barrier regulating traffic, feeling as foreign and out of place as he had on the first day, then turned into the dark archway to the English faculty building. He went up the stairs—everything was lighted up but silent. If ever there came a time in the future—say, fifty years from now—when English departments fell out of use, and no one had a clue what to do with them, so that the hallways remained illuminated but unoccupied, then *this* was what the building would look like: quiet and purposeless. First floor; second floor. The departmental office, with its door closed. On the left, opposite the common room which students darted out of and into during term, was the steady line of offices of the Renaissance scholars, Romanticists, Victorianists, and the 'twentieth century' teachers.

*

'*Come* in.'

Into the narrow but sunlit room, made somehow larger rather than smaller by the range of books crammed neatly and stood on shelves, from works first published at the beginning of the nineteenth century to a slight offering of stories that had come out a few months ago. He slipped into the armchair.

'Thank you for these,' Mr Davidson said. He was in a jacket, despite the warmth.

In his hand, a sheaf of papers—Ananda's poems. His latest ones. He'd given Mr Davidson an assortment previously, after having probed him shyly with the question, to which Mr Davidson had replied without equivocation that he'd be 'happy to see them'. Here, already, were further offspring, which he'd shared with him last week.

'I enjoyed them.'

Not so good. The term 'enjoy' was imprecise, worrying, insincerely mollifying, vaguely insulting. So it was with the last set of poems too. But Ananda had almost forgotten Mr Davidson's earlier lukewarm encouragement. Three weeks is a long time for a young poet. Memory is short; the young man is trying out various voices and registers at different moments— even different times of the day. Feeling self-importantly out of sorts in the morning, he might well write a deprecating poem in the tone of Larkin; in the afternoon, rereading one of Eliot's Sweeney poems, he could, by evening—already having forgotten Eliot, but unable to shake off that mood—produce ironic verses on sexual malaise. The twentieth century and its literature, from its birth in around 1910 to the present moment, is passing through him, unbelievably compressed, in less than a year—in spasms and transitions. So the young poet is in a state of constant inspiration. Partly this has to do with being in a condition of strange incompleteness, the twenty-two-year-old mind, acute and wide-ranging, unable to come to terms with the body's ever-returning sexual desire. Partly it has to do with the excitement of being in the midst of modernity, and of paying homage—to Larkin, to Edward Thomas and Dylan Thomas, to Eliot, to Baudelaire, to Pound, even to the poets he feels remote from, like Robert Lowell. Paying homage—that is, writing other people's poems as if they were his own—makes him, on certain days, jubilant, and gives him immense power: he is, as it were, recreating these poets at will, through his spasmodic enthusiasms; remaking what he knows as literature. In some not-irrelevant context, Hilary Burton had said to him, laughing, 'Words, Mr Sen! "*Words*, Degas—poetry is made out of words, not ideas,"' quoting Mallarme to him in a way he didn't understand, and yet digested. But it was words—their sounds, their unpredictable moods—that made him write the poems.

*

'I must say you're *virry* prolific!'

A wry holding-back, almost a caution. Nestor Davidson had a way of emphasising words to assert admiration, or cast doubt. For instance, 'very', which he uttered musically, cramping the vowel in a way that could be, depending on context, troubling or reassuring. Pointing to a paragraph that Ananda had written in an essay, or responding to something he'd said, Mr Davidson would observe: 'That's *very* acute.' A throwaway remark, but the sort that had moored Ananda, making him experience the beginnings of a pride in himself—something quite different from the natural, stubborn egotism that made him write in the first place. But 'very prolific'? He couldn't be sure if it was a compliment—or if a percentage of a remark could be complimentary, and a percentage derogatory. He could only guess at its composition. Fifty-fifty; or sixty-forty? Surely the model of productivity in 1985 was Larkin's. He knew Mr Davidson admired him. One envied Larkin his failure to be prolific. In his demonstration of emotion and range of subject-matter, Larkin followed the standard set by his productivity, of a low-key parsimoniousness. The guarded, disbelieving tone of the poems seemed connected to the personality that brought them to the world with such reluctance. Three morose, wafer-thin volumes in as many decades! Yet there was something wonderful about their antithetical efflorescence, their muted hostility to their own existence. And Ananda often wanted to write Larkin's poems—far more often than Larkin evidently did. It was possible that Mr Davidson sensed this: the convergence, in Ananda, of the instinct to recoil, to hide himself away, with a soul in spate, leaking, spilling over, overflowing eagerly in poems he wrote every week with such facility. How could he not be 'prolific'?

*

It was very quiet. Ordinarily, Ananda didn't like silence. But the unusual quiet just after midday allowed him to hear what was happening beyond, and around, the English faculty; London was busy, in a sort of counterpoint to the first floor's inactivity. What was the road behind the buildings and alleys outside Mr Davidson's window? Malet Street? Ananda had a limited confidence in his knowledge of the immediate environs.

'I *did* like these,' Mr Davidson said, nodding charitably at the typed pages he'd placed back on the table, 'but I couldn't quite bring myself to believe'—he smiled a little wickedly, but affectionately, as if assessing Ananda retrospectively from a vantage point in the future—'in their sense of pain.'

Ananda nodded, but not because he was in agreement with Mr Davidson. He was used to having his pain mocked, or overlooked. He knew how it felt to have his poems ignored or rejected (thus the polite note from *Encounter*, which he treasured, and the irritating lack of acknowledgement from the National Poetry Competition), but not slighted. Partly he stayed sanguine because Mr Davidson had been so upbeat about his tutorial essays; this somewhat (but not wholly) compensated for his inability (what else could you call it?) to recognise the uniqueness of the tranquil, frozen records of loss that Ananda had given him. 'Across the River' had come to Ananda strangely, and it owed nothing to Larkin or Eliot. He'd written it in a dream; the poem itself was dream-like. It described a boy—the narrator—trying desperately to swim across a river, possessed by some fierce but doomed urge to reach the other side. Having failed to do so (either the current's too strong, or the boy isn't an adept enough swimmer), he runs up and down the bank till, exhausted, he lies on the sand, staring at the stars. Ananda had eschewed all punctuation but the comma—twice, he'd left a blank space between one part of a line and another, to indicate a pause and a fresh beginning. Also, he'd dispensed with capital letters at the start of each line, and everywhere else for that matter. He believed he'd been able to pull this off without seeming childishly avant-garde; that he'd succeeded in turning this and the other poems he'd shown Nestor Davidson into frozen pieces of music. It was *viraha*—separation from the beloved, an idea important to Kalidas and later to the *bhakti* poets (for whom it resurfaced as Radha's perennial but unrequited longing for Krishna)— that he must have been trying to invoke. It was a concept unbeknownst to Ananda till he was seventeen; but, once he'd discovered it, *viraha* defined with more and more exactness the yearning he'd been carrying with him for years. The object of his desire was mostly an emanation rather than a specific person with a face and name (despite the fact that he'd fallen in love with his cousin two years ago)—ah, it could even be a succession of names and faces, among whom, why not, even God could be included.

*

'And I'm sure you're not as *bloodthirsty* as this poem makes you seem,' smiled Mr Davidson affably, clearly secure in the knowledge that Ananda wasn't capable of murder; now he was quoting Ananda's own lines back to him: "*and if she'd died by me, in such a way / my soul might have been satisfied*".'

Affably? But wasn't he making fun of two of Ananda's most beautiful lines? Not cruelly, maybe; but not affably surely? This poem, along with 'Across the River', he'd produced in a stupor of emotion and attentiveness to the sound of words. Could Mr Davidson, who'd been so receptive to the essays, really miss the poems' special quality? Was it because he was a fiction-writer; a different sort of beast to a poet? A novelist was about normalcy, wasn't he—and, despite his susceptibility to the reverberations of Wordsworth, Eliot, and Larkin, Mr Davidson presented the face of normalcy, of sanity, did he not? He was one who'd outlasted the first terrible pangs of love. Ananda was not only always in their throes—he couldn't seriously believe that, one day, he wouldn't be. Only two weeks ago he'd reread Auden's introduction to Shakespeare's sonnets, smiling inwardly at Auden's tentativeness, as he asserted something in a qualified manner because he *knew* it was the truth: 'Perhaps poets are more likely to experience it'—meaning 'true love'—'than others, or become poets because they have.' *That* was getting it from the horse's mouth. Mr Davidson was among those that Auden had discreetly categorised as the 'others'; the non-poets. In the quote that Auden had then offered from Hannah Arendt (once more, the apologetic air: 'Perhaps Hannah Arendt is right'), Ananda had been startled to notice his own blurred but unmistakable likeness: 'Poets are the only people to whom love is not only a crucial but an indispensable experience, which entitles them to mistake it for a universal one.' Wryly, he saw the pattern he was following, in committing a similar error with his tutor: it was no surprise, actually, that Mr Davidson hadn't grasped what the poem was doing, since, of course, he was no devotee of that 'indispensable experience'.

The poem Nestor Davidson had been gently ridiculing was a meditation on dawn (which Ananda was never up to see: all the better for his imagination and his faint memory, from childhood, of dawn's radiance); the poet is thinking of his imminent departure from his lover, while she sleeps. He'd like to hold on to that fleeting moment, as the light begins to enter the window, keep it as it is, impossibly unchanging; and this is what leads him to lyrically speculate on whether the death of his sleeping lover—because death and sleep are one—wouldn't arrest time and the day's progress; wouldn't cheat the inevitability of waking and parting. Mr Davidson's response to Ananda's tranquil, sweetly tragic mood was a blunt instrument in that stillness.

'It's a difficult art,' said Mr Davidson—now he was softly addressing himself rather than admonishing Ananda, the prose writer recalling (perhaps from experience) the mysterious pitfalls of poetry-writing. 'But what you do have is a grasp of rhythm,' he said—not grudging, but fair. 'It was *never* something I could master!' So he *had* had the experience then!—he'd given verse a go. How little Ananda knew of him—yet had reached out to him as at a straw. In a jacket photo from one of the early books, he'd been surprised to find Mr Davidson—younger, with an unbelievable moustache—smoking, the careless spume drifting away from the face. Ananda wished he hadn't seen the picture, for its strangeness but also for its supercilious but fragile optimism. He'd never caught Mr Davidson smoking. He must have given it up, as he had the 'difficult art'—or had he? Ananda decided to slip in a compliment—to prove he was superior to the little well-meaning jibes that Mr Davidson had aimed at his poems, but also to get out of his system something he'd wanted to say.

'Thank you. By the way, I liked the stories in *No Place in the Sun* very much—they're very elegantly written.' There. It was done. Something was proved.

Mr Davidson's expression changed in the summer-shadow that had alighted on the face: for less than a second, he looked haunted.

'That's *very* kind of you.' What did *this* smile, this expression mean? It was genuine happiness—held in check. 'Your opinion means a lot to me.' Ananda had had no idea. 'I'm glad.'

Ananda was glad too—a glow of satisfaction: to be regarded as an equal. *Means a lot to me*. He'd had no idea.

*

He hadn't been wholly truthful. Something was missing in the stories. What, it wasn't easy to put your finger on. Maybe it was their very craftedness that went against them, giving them the slightest hint of artificiality. But if that were really the case, the hint of the artificial was counter to the free-flowing, light style. Before he'd read the stories, it hadn't occurred to Ananda that South Africa could be written of like this—without overt politics and hand-wringing, as a landscape of sunlight, comedy, provincial drabness, and small existential dramas. Was this lack of politics a limitation: was it what made Mr Davidson a relatively minor player? Ananda could not decide. Or was it what gave to the writing its freshness and agility? Clearly, Nestor Davidson was talented. Why wasn't he better known? Ananda seemed to have a knack for becoming friendly and populating his life with people who were gifted but hadn't had proper recognition. Take his music teacher in Bombay, a remarkable singer ignored by the cognoscenti. Or his own mother, with her unique singing voice and style, of whom hardly anyone was aware. Or his mad uncle in Belsize Park, whom he called Rangamama—'colourful maternal uncle'—who shone so brightly in his youth and who Ananda's father said—quizzically, as if describing a condition—was a 'genius', but who'd imploded, arresting his own advancement. Was it something about the world, that promoted the second-rate and left the genuinely talented unrewarded; or was it something about Ananda, that he found success second-rate and spotted a gift in failures? Or—more disturbingly—was

He could be childlike with his tutor. Mr Davidson stared hard at Ananda, as if divining his fortune from his face.

'I think you have a first-class literary sensibility,' said Mr Davidson. 'But you haven't read enough to get a First.' A sudden small burst of sparrow-chatter.

'You've read far more poetry than you have prose. I'd say you've read a great *deal* of poetry.' He made it sound like Ananda had crossed a line that demarcated acceptable behaviour. 'But your reading of the novel needs enlarging.'

It was useless to deny this. Ananda loved reading poems. He avoided novels. It was a tacit—not a premeditated—avoidance. He had a restive attention span; his mind drifted when reading long books. The only novels he'd read with true gusto were those trashy thrillers he'd consumed at school. These days he read poems like thrillers. He even took them to the bathroom. Poems of a certain duration, even obscure ones, like Geoffrey Hill's 'To the (Supposed) Patron', he finished in the duration of a single crap. He then reread it, suspended over the submerged stool. He'd emerge from the bathroom in a strange mood, physically unburdened and spiritually, mentally, elevated. Of 'serious' novels, he'd only finished *All Quiet on the Western Front*, *A Farewell to Arms*, and the later, almost comical tragedies of Thomas Hardy, in which things went relentlessly wrong, as in a Tom and Jerry cartoon. Of course—being ambitious—he'd tried his hand at *Ulysses* when he was eighteen, and reached its finale without comprehending it—taking pleasure in hardly any of its features except the giant S, the first alphabet in the book. The S had undoubtedly vibrated with energy, but the book was a physical burden. He'd put it in the luggage three years ago on a trip to America with his parents, intending to examine it on his travels. A customs man at JFK had asked them to open the suitcases (in case they were smuggling in Indian fruits or sweets, perhaps). '*Ulysses*!' the large bespectacled disbelieving customs man had said. 'Are you a student?' Ananda had nodded, though he was in the equivalent of high school. '*I* wouldn't read *Ulysses* unless I was a student!' said the customs man, shutting the suitcase after his glimpse into the tantalising freemasonry of studenthood. A potentially incendiary book then—on the verge of being, but not quite, contraband. And near-unreadable. Ananda had secretly rejoiced at it being discovered in his bag on his entry into America.

*

'*Moll Flanders*,' said Nestor Davidson. 'That's the first of six novels I'd recommend you read.'

Ananda prised out a biro and his chequebook from his trouser pocket and guiltily scribbled the title on the back—in the hasty egress from Warren Street, he'd forgotten his notebook at home.

Moll Flanders! Had he read the Classics Illustrated version? Or was that *Silas Marner*? His spirits sank. So unadulteredly and classically English!

'And I think you may as well read *Journal of the Plague Year* too—it's *very* interesting.' Ananda inscribed the numeral 2 and added the name in his tiny handwriting to the chequebook's uneven surface. He had a premonition of dullness. Walls of prose.

'*Gulliver's Travels.*' What! Was Mr Davidson sending him back to school as a punishment? *This* he'd definitely encountered in Classics Illustrated, where the comedy of scale had been shrewdly exploited by the artist: the stranded, long-haired body in knickerbockers pinned to the earth— every inch of him—by minute threads. Beautifully drawn. Ananda's mother used to lovingly call him 'Lilliput' when he was a toddler. In Bengali, the word had become a noun referring not to the place but to its people. Must he now go back to this implausible giant?

Reading his mind, Mr Davidson remarked: 'Swift is the best satirist in the English language—a *bit* extreme and mad (look up "Celia, Celia, Celia shits")'—Ananda paused; then rushed to notate the quotation—'but worth your while I think. I'd add *Jane Eyre* to the list.'

Another children's book! Classic literature was what he'd encountered long ago mostly in the form of a comic book or movie; it belonged to a boy's bygone ephemera. He'd grown up; he belonged to the present; modernist difficulty was his bread and butter. He wanted no more of 'stories'. The Emmas and Fannys and Rochesters—they were of a closed English household where he'd never been welcome or at home.

87

'It's a remarkable novel,' said Mr Davidson, narrowing his eyes. The First no longer concerned him; he was trying to make Ananda look over his shoulder and notice the dim light shining in the nineteenth century.

'*Sons and Lovers*,' he said with finality. At last, a novel that didn't originate in antiquity! Bursting with sex too, from what Ananda had heard.

'That's enough reading. I'd be *very* curious to know your thoughts once you've finished.'

* * *

He was going to see his uncle. But he must get something to eat. Senate House was nearby. He decided he wouldn't. The busy dining hall on the top floor—it was far too English. The English were a strange lot: even if they didn't acknowledge your existence, they made you feel on display. How did they manage to do that? Their books advocated the virtues of observation—but they didn't look at you directly. If you sat opposite an English person, you may as well not be there— that was English politeness, or the rules of the culture. It wasn't obliviousness. They did practise the art of looking in secret; on the tube, in the silence of human contiguity, Ananda's eyes had more than once alighted accidentally on the reflection of a co-passenger, and found he was being studied. The eyes had immediately slid away, but he'd been startled that his existence had aroused curiosity. His uncle, with his misshapen racial superiority, often warned him against making eye-contact with skinheads and even punks: 'Would you look an animal in the eye? No. Because it thinks it's a challenge.'

He saw his uncle once or twice a week. They got on each other's nerves, but had grown fond of the frisson. He was Ananda's sole friend in London—and Ananda his. 'Friend' was right; because his uncle was capable of being neither uncle, nor father, nor brother. He mainly needed a person to have a conversation with—specifically, for someone to be present, listening and nodding, as he talked. When his sister and brother-in-law had returned to India in 1961, the deprivation of such a person in his life had, slowly, changed him. As his basic requirement was an avid companion, he didn't get married, because the distractions of sex and administering a family would leave less time to talk about himself. Deprivation had already turned him—when Ananda visited London in 1973 with his parents—into a hermit in a dressing-gown. The rug and furniture in the first-floor bedsit was covered with a fur-like lining. The pans in the kitchenette sink hadn't been treated to a washing liquid for years. He was cheery to outward purposes, his sideburns signifying the mood of the time, a shipping company high-flyer. When he came to see them in their hotel room on their next visit in 1979, he was bitter. For some reason, he was furious with Ananda's parents. He'd emptied the round coconut *naroo* that Ananda's mother had brought for him from home into the wastepaper basket. They placated him somehow, for the hurt they'd unknowingly caused. Because the person who congenitally seeks companionship—rather than seeking out, say, positions of influence or power—is also, often, a compulsive quarreller. There are hardly any terminal severances in his life, as he can't afford them. His relationships might be defined by discord, but they're also permanent.

*

Circling back to Warren Street, so he could pay Walia the rent, Ananda crossed at the traffic lights. He still wasn't

90

out of Bloomsbury. Discovering the college was in the heart of Bloomsbury had once compensated an iota (no more) for his misery in London, and for the fact that he wasn't in Oxford or Cambridge. The entrance exams he'd have had to take for Oxbridge—given his aversion to being quizzed and assessed—decided it for him; and the fact that he'd need to write a Latin paper for Cambridge had made up his mind. But he might still have wavered if his uncle hadn't casually said he'd put him up. Staying with him seemed like a feasible idea at the time. Another reason to be in London. How the two would have fitted into the bedsit was never put to the test. Part of the lore about his uncle had to do with how he'd taken in Bontu, an older cousin of Ananda's, when he was a poor research student at the School of Tropical Medicine. Many were Bontuda's stories about his uncle's and his odd-couple existence—till Bontu got his doctorate and escaped. Maybe some kind of wisdom made his uncle retract his original offer to Ananda. By then Ananda was already aimed for London. He didn't change direction. When he realised at last that he was almost daily in Bloomsbury, he couldn't find it. Whenever he came to college, he thought he'd encounter it without having to actively search for it. The sixties stone building of the Bloomsbury Cinema and the bed and breakfasts with black doors on the outer reaches of Gower Street didn't add up to the place.

*

Nestor Davidson's rebuttal—his misreading—of his poems was sinking in. He pondered over the remark, 'I'm sure you're not as bloodthirsty as this makes you appear,' as he walked towards Charlotte Street, feeling faintly hungry. He was unassailable. The words didn't hurt; they weren't meant to. They were a detail in a small chapter in a larger story whose shape still wasn't clear; but Ananda sensed that glory, in the end, would be his. Walia: he'd promised he'd give him the cheque this afternoon. The Natwest chequebook was curled double in his pocket, less a financial accessory than an extension of himself.

*

Down the stretch of Charlotte Street he went—he liked the route, because there was no one else on it, and he felt like he possessed the road—till he came to Grafton Way and turned right. Here was Walia's kingdom. He had two restaurants here. The one on the corner of Grafton Way and Whitfield Street was fancifully called Diwan-i-Khas, the Regal Court, as in the Red Fort, from where the Mughals centuries ago had reigned. In fact, the environs gave off echoes of Mughal imperial history, and, on Tottenham Court Road, a minute away, was the Red Fort itself, Lal Qila, a better-quality restaurant than Walia's: its tandoori quail was fabulous, though you had to take care to extricate the deceptively thin bones in the bird's flesh in case you choked on one. On Whitfield Street was (named after another section of the interminable Red Fort) a second restaurant, Diwan-i-Aam, the Commoners' Court. Ananda had presumed that this was a rejoinder by a rival to Walia, until he found that the dashing Punjabi owned both restaurants. There was a joke among tenants in the buildings Walia owned on Warren Street that, given the steady advance he was making in capturing properties, he'd become 'Lord Walia' before long. The little stretch of Whitfield Street between Grafton Way and Warren Street was not, however, salubrious. On one side lay a vacant lot behind which was a shattered building occupied illegally by people from the Caribbean—whose proximity scandalised the wealthier Indian expatriates in Walia's flats. On the opposite side was a neutral Bangladeshi grocer's, and Diwan-i-Aam (through the panes you could see customers submitting to men dressed like Peshawari soldiers), which marginally enlivened the stretch in the evening. But best was the Jamaican music shop adjoining the vacant lot, on your left if you were directly facing Diwan-i-Khas on Grafton Way. Without explanation or warning, it would sometimes vibrate with music of simple, uncomplicated joy, comprising two or three chords and an agile melody.

*

Walia was usually to be found in Diwan-i-Khas, the Regal Court; you rarely spotted him in Diwan-i-Aam. Entering, Ananda at once saw him at a table between the doorway and the bar. He was in his mid-fifties, with an air both youthful and authoritative. His sartorial sensibility had been shaped by the seventies. He wore a pale, silken shirt—its sheen achieved a kind of parity with his silver hair—and left the first two or three buttons unfastened, so that you were provided a glimpse of his largely hairless torso—with the exceptional strand of grey—and the curve where his mildly assertive paunch began. Close friends called him Manny: an affectionate contraction of Maninder. Despite his cheesiness, he stood out; he was handsome, in a Punjabi-aquiline way, his flared nostrils giving the impression of a man who had a temper and an instinct for flamboyance.

Ananda had never been a rent-payer before; Walia was his first landlord. He didn't know how to take him. Though it was well disguised—maybe even subconscious—he couldn't banish the feeling that Walia was a subordinate. An intellectual one. What was he but a small-time 'Asian' businessman, despite his airs? A man who temporarily had the upper hand. What was 'Asian' anyway—an equivocal category, neither British nor Indian, for people who had essentially nowhere to go? The whole notion of Walia's properties became a bit of a joke then, something he was making up on the hoof. Maybe these prejudices—a set of defences, really, on Ananda's part, against one who exercised power over him—somehow conveyed themselves to Walia, and explained his stiffness.

'Mr Walia.'

He looked up from whatever was absorbing him in the ledger, smiled faintly.

'Ha—how are you?'

'Fine thank you. Uh—I've got the rent.'

Not cash in hand. He dipped into the pocket for the chequebook. The rent was two hundred and fifty pounds—a hundred more than before, given the sequestering of the kitchen and the conversion of the second floor into Ananda's studio flat. Ananda's mother had had a showdown with Walia in Diwan-i-Khas about the rent and the neighbours. 'You can't charge us because other people behave terribly!' She'd flashed her big angry eyes. That usually worked. 'You don't know who you're talking to,' she said. How could he? Could he have any conception—this restaurant owner—of their apartment overlooking the sea, or her husband's exalted position? 'You're nothing,' he'd said, studying the ledger, not so much shying away from eye-contact as not troubling to look at her. 'Nothing.' She was. Neither her dominance nor her husband's extended to here. She could protect Ananda, but mainly with joking camaraderie. Later, she'd mimicked Walia—'You're nothing, you're nothing'—and they'd relished the remark. There was no change to the barely affordable rent.

*

The smell of fenugreek. A sudden hiss: someone had ordered the tandoori platter. There weren't that many people: weekday lunches were a desultory affair. Diwan-i-Khas was largely uninfiltrated. He took out the cheque, doubled foetally on itself. Smoothed it on the table.

The Sylheti waiters tarried discreetly. Benevolent backup. Walia's troops, but Ananda's kin. From the ancestral land he'd never seen.

'Kemon asen?' said the handsome one with the thinning hair in an undertone. Ananda had never forgotten him. He had the steadfastly reassuring air he'd had when, two years ago, Ananda and his parents had entered Diwan-i-Khas for the first time; once his father and mother had divulged over the beginnings of tarka daal and pilau rice that they hailed from Sunamganj and Habiganj respectively—how it had startled this man!—the subject had turned to rentable property. The hostel had become intolerable; its drunkards and merrymakers—international students—were keeping Ananda from practising music. Someone said the hostel was rumoured to be a 'pickup joint'. But Ananda hadn't been able to take advantage of that aspect of the place either. In the course of their uninformed search for alternative accommodation, they'd slipped into Diwan-i-Khas. 'Folaat?' the waiter had asked, unflappably resourceful, as he poured tap water from a jug. 'You want fo-laat?' Ananda was delighted by the neologism. It was deliberate—meant to put them at ease, earn trust in a way that English or standard Bengali couldn't. So it was when waiters were plying them with mango chutney. 'Fikol?' they'd say solicitously, holding

the bowl of mango pickle aloft, disorienting, then disarming, them. Yes, they'd have fikol, how could you demur to such a request, which admitted you to the deepest—maybe it was a slightly too deep—familiarity? 'Fo-laat?' this man hovering now by the table had said two years ago, and pointed them in the direction of Warren Street. 'Our malik Walia—he has lots of fo-laats, ask him.'

To his enquiry now, 'Kemon asen?', Ananda said, 'Well'—'Bhalo'—standard Bengali; no one, not even his parents, spoke to him in Sylheti, and he wouldn't presume to reply in it with the rustic 'Bhala', fearing it might sound like a parody of the tongue. When he was little, his parents had instructed him that Sylheti was not a language but a dialect. And when he was seventeen, he'd lighted on an aphorism by Marshall McLuhan: 'A language is a dialect with an army and a navy.' His people—if he could call these waiters *his* people—perhaps didn't have an army or navy, then? But actually they did, having wrested and carved out their land in 1971. The land that, before 1947, was Ananda's parents and theirs was now solely theirs. Still, could they be entirely happy in it if they were, today, not there, but here, at the tables of Diwan-i-Khas?

* * *

From the newsagent's—two shops to the right of Diwan-i-Khas—he decided to get his near-daily copy of the *Times*. First he passed Asian Books and Video, with its tranquil but impoverished air, like a duty-free shop in a socialist country. He'd been in there once, wondering if he might uncover some bootlegged Asian porn (he'd never seen any, it was the myth of it that was compelling) in the basement—if there was a basement. Instead he found books on agriculture, philosophy (by Radhakrishnan), religion, and stacked copies of *India Abroad*; and what looked like smudged, pirated videos of *Shaan* and *Chacha Bhatija*. He had wanted to but balked at asking the balding, good-looking, empathetic proprietor, 'Do you, by any chance, have Asian porn?' He wasn't sure at which point the empathy would dry up. But he did often feel the invisible, gravitational pull of racial empathy: that the Indian, Pakistani, black, even the Chinese, could be presumed upon in a way that the white man couldn't. The outlines of their consciousnesses were fuzzier, less individual, and softer, like their physical features—noses, jawlines, bodies. Ananda felt a strange unconscious familiarity among them—in ordinary circumstances, he wouldn't have noticed his countrymen; but he noticed them here, reviewing them not only with recognition, but with accumulated knowledge and an emotion he hadn't previously been aware of. Indeed, the very urge and temptation not to notice them—not just Indians, but the heterogeneous tribe of the non-Caucasian—to take them for granted, was something he thought of now as quite wonderful:

a gift. Before this profound temptation, and due to it, the stubborn conflicts—between Indian and Chinese, Pakistani and Indian—melted and became irrelevant. In contrast, you couldn't not be aware of a white man. His very clarity and perfection of features made each version of him separate, singular, and quietly nervous-making.

The balding man in white shirt and dandyish striped trousers inside Asians Books and Video didn't see Ananda; but Ananda glanced at him as he would at an expected landmark, put aside his need to make urgent queries, moved on towards the newsagent's. At the neighbouring shop, surveying boxes of vegetables and fruit and herbs displayed outside the steps, was shakchunni (so Ananda's mother called her; they didn't know her name); also known at different points in time as *churel* and *dain* among the neighbours in Walia's flats. She'd been consigned to the dominion of ghouls because of her ashen appearance (always wrapping her small stick-like figure in a faded printed sari) and her unhelpful personality. No longer did they go to her for yams, coriander, tomatoes, or other produce; but occasionally, when they fell unexpectedly short, they navigated her for Ribena or a carton of milk; then dealt with her eerie supernatural silence at the till. Her husband—in glasses—looked more generically human, and could even have passed for an accountant; he was no less unfriendly, but that could be because he was entrapped and, as a consequence, dour. On the other hand, shakchunni might be wasting away because of this bespectacled husband, whose very motionlessness was energy-sapping. Ananda arrived at the newsagent's, hawkishly extracted a copy of the *Times* from the rack outside, climbed up the three steps. The newsagent, Manish, like shakchunni, was Gujarati, but second-generation; 'A nation of Gujarati shopkeepers'—the joke was so obvious that, though he suspected he'd invented it, he couldn't believe it was original; a thousand people must have thought up the same line; no one ever bothered to speak it aloud because it was so silly. His Highness and Excellency Dr Rev. Sir Idi Amin had supervised the egress of the Gujaratis—mainly Patels; Manish too was Manish Patel—from Uganda thirteen years ago, leading, quite literally, to a change of colour in the English neighbourhoods. And four years before this happened, the Oracle—silver-tongued, Oxford-educated—had predicted strife in England and raved eloquently about the river Tiber foaming with much blood, a pronouncement that had been variously interpreted. 'How are you, mate?' said Manish. 'Aw-right?' He said this to Ananda each day. Sometimes it was only, 'Aw-right?' Today Ananda sensed the words expressed not a social nicety but real concern, as if Manish had a fleeting but shrewd inkling, from the moments they spent with each other, of Ananda's ever-returning homesickness and the recent departure of his mother. 'Fine thanks,' said Ananda, and Manish smiled and nodded quietly; he'd abandoned his faded maroon jumper, but the smile was, as ever, framed by the changeless hirsute growth that was neither beard nor stubble. It was Manish who'd announced to Ananda the death of the grand witch, Indira Gandhi, when he'd come in to get the *Times* at half past eleven one morning nine months ago; Ananda had overslept and had no idea the world had changed in the small hours. While making his usual pointless arc from Fitzroy Square to Grafton Way, he'd noticed the flag on top of the Indian YMCA at half-mast and was puzzled; looked back twice to check the flag, then put it out of his head till Manish, in his faded maroon jumper, told him with that same look of concern: 'Do you know Mrs Gandhi's been shot?' 'What?' 'Yes.' 'Is she dead?' 'They're not saying.' That and the next day Ananda wondered if his country would splinter at the news; and would he be stranded in Warren Street if it did? And for how long then would he have to be here? He'd never before doubted his nation and its viability. But it survived and persisted through the violence and through the seasons. Manish, a bit of a divine messenger in disguise, continued to give Ananda the latest cricket scores along with the small change.

* * *

Surya. Helios. Phaeton's dad.

The interiors of English houses weren't built to cope with uninterrupted, heat-inducing sunshine. But odd how it conferred beauty, even on these very streets—Warren, and Whitfield, Grafton Way, even illuminating Charlotte Street, which otherwise seemed permanently to be in the shade. It wasn't as if the sun was just the ruler of the universe that he, Walia, and even the Patels lived in; he was its creator—not only in sending out the ray of light that penetrated the seed and stirred the shoot. The sun wove maya—the fabric of the visible world. Some Hindus said that maya was dream, or illusion; but there was nothing else to speak of—the visible world was all there was. It was his work. Daily the enchantment recurred—except in England, not daily; there were weeks and months of anaemic reality, when the sun was reluctant, and Tottenham Court Road was an industrial version of itself. On such days, the lights of the night were more uplifting—the lamps, the lit shop windows on Oxford Street, the neon advertising—than the light of day, and you prayed for the day's end so you might seek out areas alive with artificial glitter. But today—like yesterday—the sun was out, and living as well as inert things verified his handiwork: shakchunni, the cabbages in the crate outside her shop, the newspaper rack—all were complicit in this work-in-progress: the day.

*

The English outside the Grafton Arms had taken off their shirts; expanses of pink with ruddy blotches, swigging down lager. If only they'd had more sun! This is what they'd have been like—semi-naked, sedentary, congregated in pairs or threes. They wouldn't have needed Empire—because their souls would have been full.

Alas, that's not the way history had turned out. The weather was what it was; Empire had happened; Ananda was here. Sometimes, in November, when the day shrank and grew damp, Ananda daydreamed about what it would have been like if India had been colonised by the Caribbean. He'd have been at a Caribbean university, in shirtsleeves the whole year. The thought consoled him as he made his way to Malet Street.

But that wasn't how history turned out!—which is why he was in Warren Street rather than St Kitts or St Lucia. That's why the people from St Kitts and St Lucia were here too—the little shop on the corner of Whitfield Street, with its euphoric spells of music.

Thank goodness for immigrants! They—tired West Indian women steering prams before them, Caribbean workmen at building sites, wrestling with each other during their breaks like teetering boys, Paki gentlemen in worn black suits, the sudden swarms of dark-skinned children following in the wake of a schoolteacher, even the industrious, practical, seldom-smiling Chinese—they brought some sunshine to a place starved of light. The Gujarati and Pakistani shopkeepers kept the day from sputtering out: their shops open till after nine,

His hunger had passed, but then been revived by the static of the tandoori platter. He was suddenly ravenous. Near Goodge Street there was an American Style Fried Chicken which, till recently, he was too ingenuous to realise was *not* Kentucky Fried Chicken. There was McDonald's of course—for which, he'd heard, oxen were compressed and flattened (like one of those cars pounded to a flat metallic shape in a scrapyard) to a neat patty—eyeballs and all. This horrible diminution surely offended some primordial law? Would someone pay one day?

At the Greek takeaway on Charlotte Street he paused to look at a rotating rump of meat, from which a man scraped shavings at intervals. Also, impaled on skewers were small chunks of—beef or mutton? A small flood of saliva filled his mouth. Could these be progeny of the food mentioned adoringly in the *Iliad*? Food was usually more appetising in books, and Homer's descriptions had galvanised Ananda's gastric juices—just as, when he was a boy, reading, in Enid Blyton, of picnics flowing with scones, milk, sandwiches, and jam used to fill him with a powerful longing. That surfeit was missing from the life he'd come to know in London, although, if you could afford it, you could eat halibut in a restaurant, or rainbow trout in butter and almonds. The days of rationing—which he'd learnt of from his uncle—were long over. He went in, shyly ordered a skewer of lamb from the moustached Greek. The rump on the spindle had an unpleasant smell. Chewing a dead, resistant piece, he fantasised he was partaking of the food Homer had written of—then rejected the fantasy.

3

Eumaeus

Usually, he descended two levels at Warren Street for the journey, riding escalator after escalator, ignoring the sign saying Victoria Line, reaching deeper into the earth for the Northern. Today he was near Goodge Street. He took the lift down and just missed the train when he reached the platform. There would be another one in two minutes, going to Edgware.

This was a kind of default route. He'd known hardly any other since that first visit in 1973. Belsize Park was inevitable; he and his parents went no further north—Golders Green was unexplored; Hampstead he only ever went to on foot with his uncle. And his uncle made that journey slightly melodramatic, staring portentously at Ananda—when was he ever serious?—and saying, 'The Devil lives in the North.' 'The North? I thought the Devil lives in Hell,' said Ananda, recalling, at once, his favourite line attributed to Mephistopheles: *Why this is hell, nor am I out of it.* 'The North,' insisted his uncle, 'is beloved of the Devil. They say the further North you go, the greater the chances of running into him.' The map opposite the platform depicted one straight line splitting into two, High Barnet dangling from the left, Edgware from the right—and

Mill Hill East, not far above High Barnet, appearing to hang from a hair. The picture was imprinted in Ananda's mind as the essence of an expedition. Not because he lived in Belsize Park, but because he repeatedly went there. In the train, the map of the Northern Line was drawn sideways, becoming a bracelet in two parts, united and linked together at Euston.

The bracelet's outer border—trains bound for High Barnet or going via King's Cross—were irrelevant, no, inimical, to him. Stops like King's Cross, Moorgate, and Angel had to be avoided, despite being on the Northern Line; head for them, and you were lost for half an hour. Other lines—Metropolitan, Central, Piccadilly—existed as rumour, in narratives he had little interest in.

*

Not that he had to go to Belsize Park to see his uncle. They also appointed other locations. They decided this on the phone. Neither had a phone—but this didn't deter them from calling each other. After the Patels had prised out the coin box, the payphone had become a relic without function and Ananda had to have recourse to a booth on the opposite side of Warren Street, near Tandoor Mahal. From there he called Bombay, speaking to his mother, her clear childish voice reaching him after a delay, like a benediction. When he needed to talk to his uncle, he called the neighbour, Abbas. 'One sacund, please,' Abbas said—Punjabis from Pakistan had perfect manners—and sometimes Ananda heard him knock vigorously and proclaim: 'Nandy—Nandy! *Tumhara nephew hain.*' Some expected shambling; then the baritone—'Pupu!' (Ananda's ignominious pet name.) *'Kemon achho he?'* His uncle addressed him in a lisping way—like Ananda was an overgrown child who required special handling. He usually sounded amused talking to Ananda—and surprised. He was capable of bickering with Ananda. But they might concur that Marble Arch or Oxford Street was the best meeting place, and experience a bit of satisfaction. This decision shaped the next few hours. What they did then—even if it was the same as what they did every day—would be an accomplice to their future convergence. By the time they hung up, both of them—but particularly Ananda—were fulminating; because his uncle would have complained again about a remark Ananda's father or mother had made, or something Ananda himself had said, and also offered a long, uncalled-for justification for an opinion *he'd* expressed last week. To this, Ananda had to reply with 'Okay, okay, fine'—his role being to soothe and bring closure—while secreting his third 10 p coin into the slot; when the warning beeps went off again, he'd say, 'I'm running out of change, Rangamama, we'll talk this afternoon'—giving them, before they were cut off, just enough time to rescue a semblance of good humour, his uncle his feeling of anticipation, and say provisional farewells.

* * *

The tube to Edgware was near-empty. It was that time of day. The suited yuppies would begin to enter the parted doors in a couple of hours, till there was no room to stand. But, given his daytime schedule, Ananda hardly knew rush hour. Tube-travel was spacious; he often found himself headed somewhere in the company of stragglers. 'Company' was the wrong word, because they didn't know each other. And the chances of them seeing each other again were few, if not nil. This fact underlined—without emphasis—the short journey, given the paucity of passengers. During rush hour, the passengers jostled and threatened to merge. Now, the five or six others marooned on seats brought home to Ananda the contingency of their nearness—without the thought surfacing with finality. *He* was off to see his uncle; *they* weren't. If another person or two alighted at Belsize Park, it would be intriguing to see how long their journeys coincided; eventually, the others would fall away, and Ananda's path to the basement bedsit would be his own. There was a beautiful tall girl in a black dress on the far side, who looked absorbed in everything but where she was. She denied the tube entirely. Her eyes altered direction every few seconds as she raced, very still, with some unfolding preoccupation. A Gujarati couple got on at Euston, at once mercantile and spiritual—old; managing to make their progress a pilgrimage and an enterprise. They didn't speak; they were receiving and absorbing the train's motion—but he knew by some unspecified rule of recognition that they were from Gujarat: their arrival here had been presaged by the Oracle, moving him to his 'rivers of blood' grandiloquence. The man wore a black jacket and grey trousers, the woman a pale white cotton sari; both had keds on. They were subtly wizened— Gujaratis tended to wizen gracefully, as if in preparation for withdrawal. Yet they were a worldly lot; you could sense that in the couple's wordless determination. Ananda envied this fearlessness; *he* wouldn't have had the gumption to go around in a faded sari and keds in London. Despite his pretences, he cared about what he looked like.

*

'Asians' is what the couple would be called here. Ananda didn't see himself as 'Asian'. He was keen to militate against the category, though his militancy must, naturally, remain incommunicable to the people it was intended for. He was Indian. He'd go back home some day—the deferred promise defined him. When he'd visited London in the summers of 1973 and 1979, he'd seen 'Asians' for the first time—a family in Belsize Park in particular, whom his parents knew from their time here before they'd returned. The nice Bengali bhadralok lady had a boy who was Ananda's age—eleven. He had casual long hair which fell repeatedly on his eyebrows, and he spoke exactly as a London boy would, unobtrusively dispensing many of his t's. He *was*, actually, English. Speaking the language in that way translated his features, his facial muscles, into the idiom of this city's culture. They'd run into each other during subsequent explorations in the neighbourhood that summer, but never talked again. Ananda was convinced that this was an Indian boy who *belonged* more to Belsize Park than to India; he was enveloped by a curious shyness when he saw him in the distance, and tried to avoid him.

The 'rivers of blood' speech was still quite fresh that year, and he remembered his uncle—in flared trousers, sideburns tapering down from the thinning scalp—refer to it with an impish smile. In less nice neighbourhoods, the National Front left parcels of shit on the doorsteps of Indians and Pakis. Indians had then only just emerged into this new identity— 'Asian'—from having not long ago been 'black'. In fact, his uncle still called himself 'black'—having maybe boasted of his Bengali antecedents one moment ago ('Tagore turned Bengali into one of the seven richest literatures in the world,' he'd say, citing an English scholar, not bothering to tell him what the other six literatures were). In the time of colonisation even Tagore—a veritable bearded Zeus atop Olympus—had playfully called himself 'black'. It was the convenient catch-all en masse term for those not from Europe. The Greeks, responsible for European civilisation, only barely escaped the misnomer by virtue of being lightly tanned. However, Ananda had sensed the Greeks were visible to the naked English eye from a mile off. The gradations of colour between white and black were infinite in London; you didn't *need* the seven colours of the rainbow here—these two were heterogeneous enough to suffice.

His uncle hadn't completely eschewed the word—in fact, was fairly comfortable with it—as, over time, with most of his hair gone, and given his round nose, he was beginning to look Jamaican. He'd been mistaken for a Jamaican by strangers a few times. This both amused and troubled him. 'Don't think that Africans and West Indians all look similar,' he told Ananda. 'If you study them carefully, you'll notice Ethiopians are very good-looking.' He had an agenda for race. 'Ethiopian,' he'd say under his breath when a handsome dark-skinned man walked by. Partly he continued using the word because he'd come to England when 'black' and 'white' were the only two camps in the country. Partly it was to distance himself from the Bengali bhadralok, who, with their pusillanimous ambitions (to become GPs or at the very least clerks in the railways), their small semi-detached houses in East London and their children in Westminster and Harrow, he saw as the very antithesis of himself—solitary, without roots, without family or clear future. 'I'm a black Englishman,' he'd say proudly to fresh acquaintances. He always wore a tailored three-piece suit with a maroon silk tie neatly ensconcing his collar, and a matching handkerchief in his breast pocket. The matter of colour was a joke to him, Ananda suspected—just as it was to the Africans. He'd recount a conversation he'd once had with a bunch of émigrés in 1957, his first year in London, when they were telling each other where they'd come from. One said, smiling, apologetic, 'I . . . *I* am from the "dark continent".' Western civilisation was all vanity, his uncle said to Ananda. The Africans led lives of continual irony.

* * *

The train passed Mornington Crescent without stopping. He caught a much-prized glimpse of the platform. Camden Town and Chalk Farm were dispatched easily; less than five minutes after Mornington Crescent, the train slowed down for Belsize Park. The old Gujarati in the jacket had nodded off; the woman—Ananda saw them both through the window when he got off, hurtling forth—was in a wakeful slumber, eyes deep and fixed. Gone. He went up the stairs, then past the semi-circular hatch (through which the platform from which he'd just risen was visible), with its onrush of air each time a train approached or after it departed—invisible gust, by which you knew a journey's aftermath or closeness. His uncle and he had strolled past the hatch a hundred times in their lackadaisical way: they never hurried for the trains, not even upon being warned by that warm breeze.

Through the collapsible doors on to the spherical cage, the lift. More than anything—escalator or staircase—this antique piece of ironwork was his connection to what was subterranean here. From the depths he emerged to view Haverstock Hill in the summer. At the exit, instead of weighing the zebra crossing, he turned right, passing the florist's adjoining the station, where someone behind the glass was harvesting bouquets for customers, choosing, bending, and embracing the flowers. The row of restaurants in the shade on Ananda's right-hand side appeared to regard him from an imperceptible incline. Weaving in and out of the shadows of trees planted at intervals, he crossed to the Hampstead Town Hall. Its ten steps rising to a sturdy black door, its facade of brick, red stone, and white borders, were inextricably related in his mind to the Pujas. Was it still a town hall? Or something else? The Pujas had moved to King's Cross. Yet each time he saw the building his memory summoned up two crowded occasions when he, his uncle, and his parents had come here for the festival, his uncle dawdling shyly, half-reluctant to encounter other Bengalis. They'd approached the space—thick with merrymakers—before the majestic staircases on either side, glimpsed, on the first floor, the goddess, noted the festoons of marigold, descended with the crowd to receive khichudi. The English ignored the festivities; as Forster had said, they'd never had gods, only goblins and fairies. They wouldn't know what it meant to have gods watching over you; they didn't know what to do with them. So, on the whole, they steered clear of the autumnal droves of women in saris, the men in suits, or flaunting dhutis. He turned left, down the bollarded slope of Belsize Avenue.

*

The sun fell on the opposite side of the road. He walked past the Scandinavian-type apartments as well as the spacious opening into Belsize Village; crossing as if on cue to the other side, continuing a few seconds up the road, he noted the tile that said BELSIZE PARK NW3. The houses on the right paraded themselves one after the other, the front door up a flight of steps—they were like actresses on a stage, ageless, full frontal for the audience. They had their trinkets—columns, pediments, fluted whorls. The basement was on ground level; the main house occupied a proscenium. Number 23—which was coming up—had a green door; number 24 was maroon. On the border of 23—separating the steps from what could be used as a parking space—was a very low wall, a platform you could even sit on. Through the sunlit space by it, Ananda advanced to his uncle's room at the back. There were two empty milk bottles on the ground, and a garbage bin, the plastic liner making a narrow lip under the lid. And his uncle's windows—fortified, for some reason, with bags from Budgens. He wasn't sure if his uncle ever carried a briefcase. Even when they'd twice had a rendezvous at Moorgate Station, when his uncle still worked in the 'city', Ananda hadn't seen him with one. Maybe briefcases were overrated by office-goers, and his uncle had shown that it was possible to live without them. His sole accessory as a peripatetic man was the Budgens bag. He also carried one—maybe to guarantee he'd never be short—folded in the pocket of his mac or jacket. Even when walking about with minuscule cargo, his closed fist would have penetrated the loop of the bag into the mac pocket, with it swinging idly from his wrist as he walked. He probably didn't believe in throwing the bags away just in case he ran out in the future, which is why he stuffed them against the windows. Ananda rapped on one of the sealed panes. A cat—white with patches of carpet brown—which had come to pry among the

Ananda looked around him. The centre table, or dining table, or maybe the work table—whatever it was—had chairs on two sides, one bearing a pile of books on shipping law. Noticing Ananda's beady stare, his uncle made to remove this low stack, at which Ananda pulled out the other chair and said, 'That's fine, that's fine, I'll sit here.'

He lowered himself, distrustful of the surface. He patted and slapped it. The smallish table was covered neatly with pages from newspapers in lieu of a tablecloth. There were more books on it: a familiar, creased pile of the *Pan Book of Horror Stories*, a half-open novel by Stephen King, a copy of the *Sun* that seemed to have been recently consulted, a shaving mirror. Ananda looked away. The bed was right next to him, against the wall, not properly made but not wholly neglected either, the tucked blanket that would have been pulled down slightly at night pulled up again, the sheet and pillow still bearing his uncle's impress.

Ananda could see him. He was rummaging in the kitchenette. The bedsit was divided in two: this room was three quarters of it, then came the kitchenette through a doorway with no door.

He returned brandishing a can. 'Coke?' he asked. 'I'm all right,' said Ananda: he wasn't going to drink Coke in the afternoon—it seemed like a scandalous thing to do. Ananda knew his uncle had stocked up on Coke to appease Ananda's mother—from stirrings of guilt, because he so often insulted her—ever since he'd realised that she liked the drink. 'Are you *sure?'* he asked, drawing out the word 'sure' like a melancholy Bengali syllable. Ananda kept shaking his head. 'Would you like a Jaffa cake then? *Ba* Mr Kipling-*er* almond slice?' He'd become very hospitable—not overnight, but inexorably. He had a very personal notion of hospitality, though. Having long fended for himself with only a degree of success, he threatened to rain a small range of confectionary on Ananda. This was linked to his own taste rather than his guest's (the Coke was an exception)—since he had a sweet tooth, it largely comprised cakes.

*

'Guess what I had for breakfast,' said his uncle. Although Ananda knew the answer, and knew his uncle knew he knew the answer—as he asked the question of his nephew each time they met up and the answer was the same—he pretended courteously not to know, because he knew his uncle wanted to tell him again. *Epic theatre.* The point being not to learn a new story, but to hear it, with recognition, recited for the umpteenth time. So with audiences of epic sagas, who'd been told the tale ad absurdum, knew the lines by heart, and delighted at being told again.

'Coffee with a bit of cream and eleven spoons of sugar, and a quarter of a toast with half a spoon of honey.' He looked distant and amused—his hunger had been exacerbated by his inadvertent mention of the Jaffa cakes. 'I haven't eaten anything since then. I'm burning with hunger!' He seemed pleased at his feat. Pleased, because his diet followed some theory of life—to do with subsistence, staying fit and lean (he worried uninterruptedly about how he looked), and with maximising pleasure when he ate in the evening. Even then, prolonging and deferring pleasure would take precedence over killing hunger; he'd chew with infuriating slowness, holding himself in check and wading into a tantalisingly dilatory frame of time. If Ananda were eating with him, he'd be distracted from his own meal by the strangely frustrating sight of his uncle chewing. All things by dinner were universally appetising ('I could eat a horse!' he'd say in restaurants or when he came to have dinner at Warren Street), and he'd scoff at Ananda's likes and dislikes in food as finicky. He lived life by a code of punishments and rewards, withholding from himself till he was on the edge, the subsequent act of auto-kindness then feeling like a miracle. Even his living conditions had no relation to his means, but was a deliberate act of deprivation, conditions from which he'd probably release himself one day on a whim.

'Eleven spoons!' said Ananda, disapproving—this was what he dutifully exclaimed each time. Yet he *did* rise to the bait, there was a genuine reprisal of surprise at his uncle's—his entire maternal clan's—consumption of sugar (his grandmother had died of diabetes; his aunt had it; one of his cousins had developed the juvenile variety and took daily self-administered shots of insulin). Rangamama had no sign of the disease. He looked pleased at Ananda's veiled reprimand. 'And now he'll say,' thought Ananda, '"I hardly slept last night."' Still, he felt a twinge of pity. His mother had chronic insomnia. He'd often discovered her hovering near the dining table at three in the morning. She emerged to nibble at biscuits. Ananda had it: or he wouldn't have run into his mother. He glanced at the bed. It seemed well-used, frequently inhabited. Beneath it were bottles from which he averted his gaze. They brought a urinous presence to the room, mingled sweetly with aftershave. The bottles made unnecessary that trip at two in the morning to the shared loo in the hallway. Although Ananda heated his flat to tropical levels, he knew the resistance you felt at night, in the chill, to emptying your bladder—the pressure on the sphincter muscle deepened by the very chill—he knew what it was like to coerce yourself to liberate your body from the warm cell of the tucked-in blanket, climb off the bed, drown briefly in the cold, totter to the hallway. There were few more solitary odysseys. Better to do it in a bottle. 'I slept badly last night,' grumbled Rangamama.

But he looked well-rested. 'When will you be done?' nagged Ananda. His uncle had unbuttoned his shirt, draped it over a chair. He began to dab his arm with a small wet towel. 'Haven't had your bath?' 'Bath!' His uncle, as he swept his thin arms and shoulders, demurred to the question. 'No,' he admitted. 'I had a bath last in April.' It sounded dreadful; but Ananda—when he thought of it calmly, and uncle reminded him of the fact whenever he visited. What had first set off this tireless confession of regret was the news, from three years ago, that Ananda's father Satish had become Managing Director of the company he worked in. Ananda's uncle and Satish used to be inseparable in Sylhet; best friends; classmates. Both bright sparks, but Ananda's uncle, it was conceded (by Satish in particular), gifted, maybe a 'genius' (a judgement that Ananda's uncle graciously concurred with). News came of Ananda's father's ascendancy. Ananda's uncle responded with joy. Three days later, he began to explain—and he hadn't stopped—how Anderson, the chief at Philipp Bros, had invited him to take up an 'executive directorship' a year ago, which he'd turned down. 'Executive director—a post with a directorship's prestige, but few of the responsibilities. But I said I wouldn't do it . . . What an idiot! I thought it meant I'd be travelling constantly, now to Frankfurt, now to Paris, São Paulo or Madrid. That's all I wanted once—to travel, travel, travel: the high life! By the time Anderson asked me, the job had no charm any more. Idiot!' He was buttoning his shirt. In the winter, he'd wear the three-piece suit over the pyjamas—they kept him warm and were preferable to long johns. Now he made, again, his usual exculpatory statement: 'I couldn't have done it anyway. I can't start work without going to the toilet. *Not* evacuating your bowels—and drinking milk—may lead to you breaking wind at any time . . .' Ananda ruminated on this, one of his uncle's many diagnoses to do with navigating your path through a day; was reassured that he abhorred milk. 'In the office, I seldom went to the toilet to do the big job, in case someone outside the cubicle heard me breaking wind.' He made a face to indicate that that would have been a calamity. Then narrowed his eyes, conceding he was over-sensitive. But he was also hinting at the stubbornness of the powers-that-be, that rule our lives and the universe. The gods. Aeolus. Wind. Had disrupted his progress. No point harping about it—he'd been made redundant after all. Or asked to take voluntary retirement if you preferred. All this business about directorship was, as they say, History: a record of events that can be resurrected only in the telling. 'Excuse me, Pupu,' he said.

* * *

He'd gone. To do the small job. A voyage out with Pupu was a thing of joy, and he didn't want it spoilt by an urge to pee coming over him. Once it did, he'd be seized by it. So now he was in the loo, wringing himself dry. It took minutes. And patience.

It was notable that heroes in Europe had no bodily functions as such—or encumbering relatives. Neither Hercules nor James Bond for that matter interrupted their antics and missions because they had to visit the toilet. When morning came, they didn't bother to brush their teeth; they jumped out of bed in pursuit. For Bond, saving the world took precedence over everything. The furthest he went towards his hygiene was shaving, an exhibition of his pheromonic powers which was rudely cut short (depending on context) by a deadly insect, a treacherous consort, or a Soviet spy. So, even this one recorded act of his humble daily toilette was made tantalising by being never completed, and Bond was seen, again and again, brusquely wiping off what remained of the lather with a towel. This detail both unsettled and inspired Ananda and his uncle; they, namby-pamby Indians, would have assiduously washed the lather off their face before drying their cheeks. Bond had no time for niceties. Nor did he have an aunt or father calling him on the phone in the midst of his fights, or demanding to know where he'd gone in the last seven days. It was a peculiarity of Western culture: this immersion in individuality, and the pretence that haemorrhoids or family didn't undermine or subvert the frame of action—it was what made its myths so free-floating and fabulous. And this transcendence was what shaped the colonial project: *they* simply wouldn't have conquered the world if they'd paused to brush their teeth or vanished to do the 'big job'. The latter, Ananda was pretty sure, was the reason there was no Bengali Empire.

*

Although his uncle had embarked on his great journeys in the forties and fifties—Sylhet to Shillong, Shillong to London, and from being a school matriculate working as a part-time used-car salesman in Shillong to a full-fledged Chartered Shipbroker who ended up as a senior manager at Philipp Bros—in spite of this, the grand journey he focussed on daily was an internal one. Not psychological, not inner; internal. To do with encouraging the food he'd taken the previous day to make its proper, unfettered way through oesophagus, alimentary canal, intestines, and colon to its final and complete escape, helped along by violent tides of water. For, in the morning (Ananda knew), his uncle, after his breakfast of syrupy coffee and half a spoon of honey and a quarter of toast, would drink ten glasses of water to cleanse his organs and send the waste within on a burst of energy to its bigger journey. 'He's going to come back now and boast about the water he drank today,' thought Ananda.

*

Next to the doorway to the kitchenette was a splendid calendar of Kali.

Ananda didn't bother to check if it was out of date. Things were often displayed in his uncle's room after they'd served their function. For instance, the bedsit upstairs, which the landlord had now acquired for a two-bedroom conversion, where Ananda's parents used to live in the fifties, and which his uncle had inherited after they'd vacated it in 1961, to return to India. Ananda's first visit to 24 Belsize Park in 1973 also saw his entry into his uncle's former first-floor abode—for some reason, his memory would sometimes tell him it was Christmas. But it was August; he had vivid recollections of the summer; consecutive days of sunlight. Why Christmas? He now knew: the Christmas cards on the mantelpiece, and especially the cards hung sideways from a cord strung across the room, with pictures of snowmen, holly, Madonna and child, their bright fins pointing downwards. Not just last Christmas's cards, but earlier ones too—that August, Ananda found them in their assigned places, as if they'd just arrived. They were never removed, only added to.

*

Ananda went into the kitchenette to look for a clean glass. The two on the shelf had no smudges. He turned the kitchen tap, filled one, drank.

The gas cooker was unlit. The moment the temperature

fell, two hobs would burn with low flames and have faintly simmering saucepans of water on them. The vapour was meant to counter dryness. The electric rods in the other room, which became incandescent and orange in the winter, made his uncle's skin dry anyway. On the left ankle, he'd scratched a vertical gash into the skin. Even now there was a saucepan on a hob with a low still pool of water in it, its sides whitened by evaporation. Also a frying pan half full of liver, in which the sauce had congealed richly.

Plonking the glass into the sink, Ananda returned to the table and saw the *Times*, which he'd bought less than an hour ago and as good as forgotten. He picked it up and turned it round, and was gripped by SHAHNAWAZ BHUTTO SHOT. Tragic family. Enemies of India; Zulfikar had been to the same school as he, but decades before. The school was proud of the fact; the Principal, peering at them over assembly: 'Who knows? One of you might be a future Prime Minister,' while they fidgeted. Or maybe 'proud' wasn't the word, given the war in 1971. But who, in death, can be classed as friend or enemy? *I am the enemy you killed, my friend. Let us sleep now.* Was Shahnawaz with his father today? Ananda put down the paper and went for the *Sun*—astonished this time by the starved figure of Rock Hudson, smiling. This unspeakable affliction, coming out of nowhere! The gods' retribution for human happiness. He was mortified, when he turned to page three and paused over the girl's gleaming nipples, trying to feel some desire. The breasts sloped down meekly; the face was audacious and common—the sort you'd have glanced at twice in Sainsbury's and maybe made eye-contact with. This sense of possibility excited him—it was less a visual than a brazen verbal statement, more bold and shameless than anything the photograph actually contained: he was appeased she wasn't model-like, but so living, contemporary, and English—truly 'your girl of the day'. Shahnawaz Bhutto and Rock Hudson dissolved into a retrospective glimmer; empathy deserted him; his cock stirred. His uncle returned; he swiftly returned the *Sun* to the table.

'Pupu *he*,' said Rangamama. 'I'm ready when you are!' Ever the gent. Apparently he'd been miserable when he'd arrived in 1957, tearful, and wanted to run back to Shillong. 'Can I have the rabbit?' he'd said to the man taking orders in a tea shop. The man had contemptuously cast a plate of thinly sliced cheese toast before him and said, '*There's* your rabbit!' Rare-bit. Ray-bit. He was over all that now, not quite integrated but perhaps as assimilated as he could be in any milieu. Actually, he was much happier than Ananda had seen him even two years ago. The early retirement had freed him utterly. He poked at the knot of his tie and considered the face in the shaving mirror—eyes narrowed, cheeks sucked in. He had the thinnest moustache above his upper lip, which he must have cultivated as an addition when he was a youthful dandy; lips that veered towards the thin, but were a bit fuller than Ananda's mother's; a prominent nose. He didn't have fat cheeks, but some nervous anorexic impulse made him suck them in when he regarded himself, since his ideal, when it came to the ur-male, was Humphrey Bogart: urbane, dissipated. Each time he turned to the mirror he made a face like Bogart did when Lauren Bacall had just lied to him, or when he'd heard a funny sound: on high alert; undeceived.

Tearing himself away from his image, he said, 'I had ten glasses of water this morning. Flushes the system. You should try it.' A challenge. Ananda nodded vaguely.

Glancing at the broadsheet folded on the table, he wrinkled his nose: 'I never read the "intellectual" papers—*Times*; *Guardian*. I prefer the *Sun*.' A put-down—aimed vaguely, but unmistakable. The inference was: he was too good for the *Times*. Either dirt or the heavens for him: nothing in between. Ordinary mortals, belabouring their thoughts and emotions (the word 'intellectual' was a euphemism) read the *Guardian*—solitary, stratospheric wayfarers who made their own road couldn't be bothered.

Ignoring him, and still seated though his uncle was ready to go, Ananda said, as if reminding a schoolboy of his botched-up homework: 'What's that in the kitchen? You've been cooking?'

'Liver,' said his uncle, happy to share his recipes: 'Cooked with butter and onions and chilli powder—and in its own blood.'

Ananda made a face.

'That sounds . . .' He didn't need a word.

'I never wash the blood away. Arrey baba, *that's* where the strength lies.' Nothing he did was merely sloppy, though his home, his bed, his knick-knacks might make you think otherwise; everything was a product of painful strategy. One of his ambitions was to have a healthy and worryingly long life. ('I'm going to be a hundred—at least,' he'd said to Ananda, making the young man anxious at the prospect of his uncle being around for another forty years: for some reason, though he'd deny this, he took his uncle's remarks with immense seriousness.) The ambition seemed curiously at odds with his other one—of never to be born again—though there was no actual link between the two. You might want to live inordinately long; you might also wish to never experience life again. ('I couldn't stand it a second time,' he'd confessed to Ananda with an intake of breath. The word *abar*—'again'— was full of terror. 'A horrifying thought.')

The injunction about cooking liver fell on deaf ears. Ananda stayed with his uncle's statements a few moments at a time; engaging with them led to long-drawn-out quarrels.

'Give me a minute,' Ananda said, getting up. 'I'd better go to the loo too.'

'For big job or small?'

Ananda didn't give him the satisfaction of an instant reply.

'Small.' He closed the door to the bedsit behind him.

He was more like his uncle than he cared to know. *Naranang matulakrama*, his mother had said mysteriously when he was quite young: 'Man's made in his maternal uncle's mould.' Ananda's father too had pointed out resemblances, mildly surprised, as when a memory not only returns to you but is reincarnated uncannily. There were few likenesses between uncle and nephew except the slight slouch while walking; Ananda looked more like his father. But part of the DNA had been reproduced invisibly. Elements of the repetition made Ananda's parents smile conspiratorially, given the gifts Radhesh had had; but also fret, since he'd taken his peculiarities too far. The intensity of those peculiarities had hopefully been diluted in their son. Still, he had to pee before he went out—it was like the physical equivalent of a confession before dying: meant to make the journey lighter. In the hallway, entering the loo, he saw the door to Shah's room ajar. A pigsty. Made his uncle's room look tidy.

A cigarette butt! In the pool inside the commode. He knew his uncle had thrown it there. Rangamama had cut down on his smoking, but he must have one on the toilet seat. A habit acquired in Sylhet, where the bathroom—according to him—was a purgatory, the cigarette the only means at hand of negating it. Ananda flushed, a god unleashing the elements; there was a storm within, culminating in a vortex. What's this? The damn thing had survived! There it was, motionless, barely mindful of the deluge that had just covered it. As the cistern filled, he aimed his stream of urine at it and simultaneously flushed again, so that it was assaulted on both sides. The world slowly returned to what it was. What! Still there, ever-resurfacing, plucky, bothersome! He zipped his trousers. Let his uncle and Shah and the other neighbour (whoever he was; there was a third tenant in the basement) deal with it.

*

Voices. He opened the door and found Shah, tall, wearing his tweedy green jacket, addressing his uncle.

'Why you are not taking him back?' he asked the moment he saw Ananda. 'Take him to India. I told your mother the same thing!'

Shah was not his real name—it was Abbas. A Pakistani who owned a shady pharmacy in Kilburn (his uncle wasn't sure if it existed), and boasted he knew Margaret Thatcher, Michael Heseltine, and various leading lights of the Tory party. 'You want to meet Vice Chancellor?' he'd said when Ananda had murmured something about his college. 'I will arrange it.' Not 'can', but 'will'; as good as a threat. He was not only his uncle's neighbour, he was his principal 'contact'—his uncle's chief access to the British State. If, notionally, his uncle got into trouble with the government, Abbas would 'take care' of the problem. Till then, Abbas's mettle as a fixer in the higher echelons didn't need testing. Ananda had warned his uncle that it was Abbas who might get in trouble with the government soon, and his uncle might be summoned. 'Be careful,' he said. 'Shah' was the name that his uncle had conferred on Abbas as he was a dead ringer for the Shah of Iran. They referred to him in private as only 'Shah'—not even 'the Shah'. Abbas had no idea. Take away the warm, clanging Punjabi accent and put him in a white jacket with epaulettes and a cross-section of medals, and he could pass for the disgraced monarch. Or put the Shah in a tweedy jacket and you'd have Abbas. His uncle and he had been neighbours for fifteen years. On Ananda's first evening in London in 1973, when he and his parents had walked from the bed and breakfast under sodium vapour lights to an Indian restaurant on Haverstock Hill, his uncle had informed them, as they sat at a table in front of a huge picture of the Taj Mahal, 'Shah will be joining us, he lives in 24 Belsize Park,' adding by way of explanation, 'he looks exactly like the Shah of Persia.' In fact, he *could* have been the Shah (he'd joined them shortly, sidling his way into their company, his massive aquiline nose hovering in Ananda's line of vision all evening) in hiding in London, incognito in a first-floor bedsit in Belsize Park, except the Shah wasn't then in exile, but lording it over Iran with the help of SAVAK. And he might be the Shah now, except he couldn't be—the Shah had died a homeless and kingdomless man in Egypt five years ago. So this person *had* to be Abbas, living in what Ananda had noticed was a pigsty.

'You take him back, please!' insisted Shah strenuously. 'He is living here for *too* lahng. Someone will look after him better there—no?'

'Tu isskoo kyu pagal karta re,' his uncle admonished his friend, appearing displeased. He lapsed into Hindi sometimes when speaking with Shah. For no good reason: to become,

briefly, a man of the people. Also, playing the fool? One should never discount that.

Shah was making a big demonstration of his eagerness to let go of Rangamama: underlining the fact that he didn't own him. For he sensed that Ananda's mother viewed him with reserve and suspicion. He was a small, unending drain on Rangamama's funds. They knew this from Rangamama's grumblings. Of course, he also pointed out that Shah was a benefactor and help, in offering to not only shop for the groceries but insisting he do so: 'Why you are going to Budgens Nandy—I know where there are best prices for courgette and garlic and *alu. Woh tum mujhpe chhod do.*' And then he'd procure garlic, alu, unsalted butter, and a cauliflower for six pounds, pointing out: 'Very good cauliflower—you will not see so good every day.' Ananda's uncle didn't have the gumption to quiz Shah about his bookkeeping, and obediently agreed about the voluptuousness of the cauliflower. But his discontent festered. Last month, he'd parted with two hundred pounds in small payments and change to his neighbour (his own bookkeeping was laborious, impeccable, if futile), a figure that agitated Ananda's mother, since it was more than what he sent many of his relatives in Silchar and Shillong. Yet, despite his moaning, he resisted alterations to the arrangement. He valued Abbas. Also, doling out money was, today, his one way of reminding himself and others of his special status—that he was unattached; living in a bedsit more or less for the rent he'd paid in 1961 (eighteen pounds);

and the recipient of a huge pension of twenty-four thousand pounds that increased each year and was also index-linked (as he'd informed Ananda) to inflation. This was not including the early retirement lump sum he'd been gifted on saying goodbye to Philipp Bros. So, though he had no property to his name, no car, you could almost claim he was—rich. Except to the few who knew him (Shah was one who'd have known, his uncle must have boasted about the salary and pension to him often), it would have been impossible to know he'd had professional success—not because that was his intention, but given the kind of person he was—so that, once, when he was weaving his way in his black mac down Belsize Avenue (he'd narrated this with disbelieving delight: it spoke to him to the core), a kindly lady had startled him by giving him a pound.

*

Before Ananda's father sailed to London in 1949 to become a Chartered Accountant, he'd proposed to his best friend's sister, using him as a via media. There were two schools of thought about how this came about. Rangamama had claimed to Ananda that he was having a conversation one day with Ananda's father about Khuku: 'She's twenty-three years old, and there's still no sign of a bridegroom.' Their father had died when they were little; the family wasn't well off. Ananda's father had looked thoughtful and said: 'Don't worry, Radhesh.' The proposal followed. According to this account, the marriage was a result of Ananda's uncle's intervention, his willingness, even, to set aside his dignity. The other version of events came from Ananda's mother, who told him that, soon after their wedding in London, his father had said to her: 'It was after I heard you sing *Ore grihabashi* that I decided.' 'But that was long ago!' 'That was when I knew . . . a person who sang the way you did had to be a good person.'

Before this, though, there was the six-year wait between proposal and marriage, Shillong and London. Khuku waited. But there seemed no guarantee that Satish would return. By the sixth year, she was close to despair. She sent him a letter, asking him to either release or marry her. She was by now twenty-nine. Satish woke up. He made arrangements for her to fly to London on an antique plane (that is, the plane imagined by Ananda was antique and industrial). One detail she repeated with satisfaction: that, because her family wasn't well off, she insisted on setting out without the gold jewellery customary to a wedding. They were married.

Soon after the wedding, she and Satish began to plan what to do with Radhesh, a genius but quite mad, who'd done so well at school but sabotaged his matriculation finals and still stood twentieth in Bengal. Early on, Radhesh had revealed a tendency to manufacture his own impediments. After he bounced back from his school debacle and stood First in his Intermediate finals, he grew obsessed with syphilis. He was convinced you could catch it from any surface, and could hardly study because he couldn't bear to touch the pages of his textbooks in case they carried the bacterium. In his attempts not to get infected, he turned each page by clasping it between his fingernails. Ananda's father noticed his friend's adoption of these methods, and the ensuing paralysis in his revision. Radhesh didn't appear for his finals; he became a used-car salesman. Even today, he was relieved, in spite of everything, never to have caught syphilis. He said so to Ananda, when he implied he was still a virgin—a fact Ananda was aware of, having heard it from his aunt, to whom his uncle had confirmed it in 1965. There had been no developments since then. Syphilis was just one reason for this state of affairs; but an important one. 'Imagine,' he'd said to Ananda, 'if you'd had sex with someone'—his 'you' was general but also pointed, and Ananda felt a personal unease at the pronoun—'and then, every time you felt a burning sensation when you passed urine you wondered—Could I have caught something?' He'd shaken his head in horror as they went up Belsize Lane and Ornan Road in the direction of the Trust House Forte Hotel. 'That's why things are so vivid and black and white to you,' said Ananda, bringing his hunch out into the open. 'Because you've never had sex. You live in an innocent complete world—it's possible for you to be idealistic. Once you've had sex, the world goes grey.' He spoke this piece of wisdom from having twice had—to his growing sense of self-torture—coitus with prostitutes in rooms in Apollo Bunder. His uncle, puzzling over the insight, bowed his head.

*

'There's no point him coming here to do Chartered Accountancy,' Ananda's father had said to his wife. 'There are too many people doing Chartered Accountancy. Let me check the situation with aeronautical engineering.' That was an idea planted in Radhesh's head by a garrulous older cousin in Sylhet. 'You'll be structuring the new aircraft,' the cousin had told him, 'both fighter and commercial. It's an international field, and given it's peacetime the arsenals for both war and commerce are going to thrive.' 'Since I have a head for numbers,' Radhesh had solemnly written from Shillong, 'I might stand a chance: calculus and algebra are indispensable here. Queen Mary College, Imperial, Newcastle are places to consider'—the names of institutions known to him from early youth coming to him with facility. But his friend thought Radhesh would prosper more in finance than in designing; he did some research and discovered that Chartered Shipbroking might be the most profitable—albeit a testing—option for the future: a cabal guarded by the near-unleapable hurdles of exams which, however, Ananda's father believed his perverse but ingenious old friend would be able to penetrate. So he pulled Radhesh from the air, and placed him in, or at, sea.

*

Khuku and her husband had lived as a couple in Belsize Park for two years; now, there was a third. Radhesh didn't live or sleep in their pockets; but almost. They'd arranged for him to live in the bedsit opposite. (After Ananda's parents' departure, Radhesh moved to *their* bedsit, and, in a few years, Shah rented *his*.) Ananda's mother ensured the friends focussed on exams while she handled the universe. Back from work at the naval department, she sometimes made bhaja mooger daal, roasting the pulses, lastly pouring in the oil, which had just popped with cardamom and cinnamon bark. The aroma was an announcement that Radhesh must cross the hallway and join them for dinner. She and her husband introduced Radhesh to herring, which she cooked in a gravy of mashed green chillies as a substitute for *ilish*. It was no ilish; it had hooped bones and none of the quills embedded in the Bengali fish. Its taste was less dark. Yet eating herring was a minor celebration, a return to the habits of home, and they made smacking noises as they sorted the bones with their fingers.

*

In both Belsize Park and Belsize Village there was a contingent of Bengali men and women. They'd come for medicine, accountancy, surgery, librarianship, and law. The scents Khuku released into the building often transfixed them. They were also intrigued by the regime and discipline she'd imposed on her husband and brother. For these people, Belsize Village and Park were at once a crowded bhadralok village and an island: from which return was desirable but not imminent.

It was as if nothing mattered—not even exams—before the urgency of gossip, food, and each other's aspirations. They were audible to one another on Belsize Avenue through half-open windows. Khuku had heard of them when she was in Shillong; a childhood friend of hers had grandly shared a letter written by her husband, already entrenched in Belsize Park and appearing for certified accountancy exams: 'I am eagerly awaiting your arrival. There are a few things you need to know about this country. You will not find it necessary to say "Thank you" here. "Q" is sufficient.' Neither Khuku nor her husband nor Radhesh wanted to associate closely with this assortment of types—to be stuck on an island punctuated by convulsions of rote-learning and dominated, between 1955 and 1961, by a mixture of restiveness and forgetfulness. By the time Ananda visited the area in 1973, the island had largely vanished. Belsize Village remained—and his uncle.

*

They were three. But who was the third? Was Radhesh Ananda's father's best friend, or had that role been appropriated by Ananda's mother? Khuku and Radhesh themselves had been exceptionally close in Shillong—in those two years after Partition, when the family had been transplanted to that hill station (its weather a preparation for, and a lesson in, English weather), they were inseparable and went for long walks up and down the hills around the lake—mistaken by some, to

The first of the Chartered Shipbrokers exams came and went. Radhesh didn't take them. He hadn't studied enough. He was fundamentally superstitious; not only in ordinary ways, but in believing that certain procedures needed to be followed to the letter before success could be ensured. In his case, the ritual was absolute immersion in preparations. He'd once passed through a utopian phase in school, when he decided that anything less than perfect preparedness was useless. This was a consequence of running into his science teacher on the street prior to his Chemistry exam, when he'd enquired politely: 'Sir, how do I ensure that I'll do well?' The teacher said, 'You should know every word in your Chemistry textbook' and went on his way. So Radhesh set about familiarising himself with each word. He never appeared for the Chemistry exam.

Ananda's father speculated about whether he'd repeat those tactics in London. But he did write his Part One the next time he had an opportunity; he passed, without distinguishing himself. He was troubled; his ambitions were aimed much higher. He'd crammed shipping law like a fanatic for six months.

Radhesh thought it over and changed strategy. Clearly, identity was key. Chartered Shipbroking was well known for being a white man's domain. They wouldn't let just anyone in, especially to the pucca upper strata. The Fellowship was fiercely competed over by men from Harrow and Rugby. Radhesh considered his surname—Nandy Majumdar. A double-barrelled kayastha title of (he liked to boast to Ananda) had left twelve years before, his father, instead of going up the steps to press the buzzer, cried in the sunlit space to the first-floor window: 'Radhesh?' The heavy window creaked onerously as it was lifted; his uncle peered out. 'Open the door!' The three went up the steps and united on the porch, as if posing for a family photograph. Radhesh, lurking inside in his dressing gown, opened the door a few seconds later. Through it they passed into the dark stairwell, and up the wide stairs on which the electric light shone a minute at a time. The house closed upon Ananda in a years-old smell of dust and curry. In Rangamama's bedsit, nothing had been polished or dusted for a few years at least. Things had multiplied: pots, cups, pans; greeting cards. Telephone numbers, including country codes (Ananda's father's among them), were inscribed in a large clear hand above the mantelpiece. (That bedsit had pink wallpaper.) A pile of the *Pan Book of Horror Stories* occupied the rug near the bed. Dust had settled in an ashen nuclear winter on the table and chairs, and formed serpentine moustaches on the sides of walls. Ananda's uncle held forth, the perfect host. The bed was unmade; he hadn't pulled up the blanket or smoothed the sheet. Ananda's father instructed his wife and Ananda to step through the windowsill on to the half-octagon of the parapet. With barely room to sit, they looked out at the breadth of Belsize Avenue, talking, Ananda glancing now and then over his shoulder. His uncle, standing in his maroon dressing gown, was declaiming, releasing statements pent up for years. His father, dressed in a suit as if

Over the three weeks of their stay, his parents used the bedsit as a watering hole, though it was more hole now than watering hole. Between the guest house with its unfriendly breakfasts and the comforts of the Trust House Forte Hotel (to which they moved after ten days), with electric kettle and tea bags, this was a place to come back to. Late one morning, Ananda and Khuku arrived at the house to find a semi-familiar smell wafting down the stairs. His uncle was cooking; when they walked in, he lowered the flame and let the gravy simmer. He'd produced a light, turmeric-and-spice-based curry of marrow and shrimps. Ananda had never had this vegetable before, but was won over by the curry's delicacy, the fortuitous neighbourliness in it of shrimp and marrow. It was served from one of those suspect saucepans. His mother resumed cooking too—dressed in a red printed sari, serving up *coder jhaal*. Thick white rectangles of cod in a gravy of chilli powder, with a spattering of turmeric, slivers of onion and fingernail shavings of garlic, and specks of *kalonji* that she'd brought from India. Amassed in a small frying pan.

*

He was briefly given reign of Belsize Village. At home, his mother never let him out of sight without a servant, but now she sent him forth on an errand: to buy a carton of milk and some salt. The village was really a square lined with shops and restaurants (including an Indian one called Beer and Curry), which, in Ananda's mind's eye, swelled, as he turned left from Belsize Avenue, like the letter omega, Ω, with Belsize Avenue forming the baselines. The shop was at the upper end of the horseshoe.

Once inside, the chocolate mousse in the freezer caught his fancy. He took it home along with the salt and milk. In the bedsit, Ananda, in his impatience, prised open the lid holding the container upside down, letting its contents fall intact on to the rug—which was, despite Ananda's father's efforts, dark with dust. The dessert was irretrievable.

*

Given this bedsit was where Ananda's parents had lived prior to his birth, the room had the air of belonging to a story. The fact that he'd heard the story several times didn't make the bedsit better-known to him. For it was very real, and difficult to make your way around in without colliding into something. Also, the neglect it had absorbed in the twelve years since his parents had gone to India gave it a touch of the unexpectedness associated with the *mamar baadi*, the 'maternal uncle's house', a place traditionally lacking in restrictions for the nephew.

By the time of that holiday in 1973, Ananda's uncle's world-conquering glory had dimmed; he was bored of it too. Radhesh had proved he was capable of great conventional professional success; but it looked like he wasn't *interested* in great conventional professional success. What he was interested in was company and family: as if responding to this in a corrective way, he lived alone and in the proximity of people who until recently were strangers. On the first floor, he had two neighbours: Abbas, and Pinku Chaudhury, a phlegmatic East Bengali who worked for British Rail and who possessed an idiot box. Radhesh made infrequent visits to Pinku Chaudhury's bedsit to watch wildlife programmes, to admire, over an hour, the tiger's stride and gathering pace, and to bemoan the gazelle's spry but fatal ingenuousness. As if in reciprocity, Pinku Chaudhury's cat habitually invaded Radhesh's bedsit, pushing its way in through the heavy door, which was often kept ajar, and jumping on to the armchair: an indolent feline with a thick brandy-cream coat and a lingering air of entitlement. He was called Vodka, and Ananda would find him politely prowling the bedsit that summer. He saw him again in 1979, but not after. When Council work began on the first floor, Pinku Chaudhury moved to Chalk Farm. Only Shah and Ananda's uncle relocated to new rooms in the basement.

*

Rangamama would encourage Ananda to sing as they went for walks that August. He'd contribute snatches in his baritone. Cliff Richard was on his uncle's mind—'He has a lovely voice,' he said, and, appropriately for the season, sang the opening lines of 'Summer Holiday' as all four of them proceeded on the pavement. Satish had bought his son *Best of the Bee Gees*, with its mustard-yellow cover and figures in Mount Rushmore-like array. Ananda already knew 'Holiday', and he approximated Robin Gibb's plaintive, melodious, nasal cry. His uncle answered with 'Bachelor Boy', humming, 'Happy to be a bachelor boy until my dying day', without Ananda sensing the irony that made his uncle's voice float unsteadily before going silent. Nor did he get the irony when his uncle ebulliently urged him to do a repeat of 'I'm going to marry in the morning, ding dong the bells will chime' as they walked up Belsize Avenue to Haverstock Hill—Ananda's falsetto standing in for the scoundrel Dolittle's guttural announcement.

*

That was the happiest he'd seen his uncle—though Rangamama had told Ananda that he'd never known happiness unmixed with disappointment. By then Rangamama was already developing his most abiding obsession—the nature of the afterlife; how and why souls come to the world, and what they do when they leave. Its main sign were the several volumes he had of the *Pan Book of Horror Stories* series. The tales in these books underlined the fact that life played savage tricks on you, that there were people out there who were suffering for no reason, and others whose sole function was to make people suffer. This, according to the *Pan Book of Horror Stories*, was what existence was, before the blank panacea of death came, and it was a world view that was then—and even today— imbibed nightly by Ananda's uncle in his bed.

He began to spend more time at Philipp Bros than at home. He did other people's work: specifically that of two juniors in his department, Paul Middleton and Freddy Gamble. His heart went out to Freddy Gamble, a timorous man, thin as his tie, who failed miserably at what he did, was newly married, and on the verge of losing his job. When Ananda and his parents saw Radhesh in 1979, Freddy Gamble was on his lips, like a backward but beloved child. In those years, Ananda's uncle returned to Belsize Park well after midnight. It was during these depressed and solitary journeys that he gradually became aware of ghosts and spirits. Once, stepping into the lift at 3 a.m. after hours of work, he felt a draught within. But where could the draught come from? He knew from his reading that a momentary drop in temperature meant a spirit was near. When it happened another night, he asked an employee in the building about it. He learned from him that there had been a death in the building on the fourth floor, seven years ago. At 2 a.m. one night, making his way back from office (he'd walked from Moorgate to Swiss Cottage), he noticed, climbing the incline between Finchley Road and Belsize Avenue, a man approaching from the distance. Which *sane* person would be out at this hour? As the strange man came closer, Radhesh, terrified, said: 'Would you like a light?' 'Believe you me,' said his uncle to Ananda, 'that man was not alive. His face was a death-mask. He had no idea of my existence. And do you know what happened next?' Ananda knew it well, since his uncle repeated the story every week, but his uncle wasn't waiting for his response. 'I walked a bit further, thinking, *Thank you, dear God, I live to see another day!*— when (I was curious) I glanced over my shoulder. Do you know what I saw? *The man had stopped and was looking straight at me.* Yes, I should have run (though what use is flight from such a being?), but was paralysed and couldn't move. The man began to make large strides towards me. I watched him, agog. *Certain death*, I thought . . . When he was face to face with me he turned sharply to his right and stared at a rusty stain on the wall. He stood like that for half a minute and then very decisively pressed his handkerchief against the stain. Then he turned around as if it were no longer of any interest to him and went back in the direction he was earlier headed.' 'Finchley Road?' 'Finchley Road—or maybe Swiss Cottage.' It was a terribly boring ghost story, made enervating by repeated rhapsodic recitations and also the fact that there was no proven ghost in it. But for his uncle it was his one episode involving what he took to be a given: the posthumous and the undead. The man was dead, the man was dead, the man was dead. It had happened, it had happened, it had happened—once. For Ananda, the tale embodied his uncle's final years at Philipp Bros: a time alternating between self-inflicted assignments undertaken on behalf of Freddy Gamble and Paul Middleton, and late-night or early-morning visions

4

Uncle and Nephew

Having shaken off Shah, they emerged from the left-hand passage of 24 Belsize Park. It was 4.20 p.m. Through the chestnut trees fell shadow-spots. 'Shah is an old soul,' observed Ananda's uncle as they progressed to the rise towards Haverstock Hill. 'Old and tired.' 'Old soul?' said Ananda. 'Yes, born into the world again and again and again. Most Indians and Pakistanis are "old souls". They've been born so many times that they're tired, they've returned to reality so often they take it for granted. If you ask Shah, "I gave you ten pounds yesterday for some cigarettes—what happened to the change?", he'll look astonished, and say, Arrey Nandy, I gave it back to you in the afternoon, because he thinks he did. He's been around for a very, very long time. Small inaccuracies escape him, and minor discrepancies don't matter. Similarly, if you ask an Indian on the street, "Bhai, which way to Camden Town?", he'll give you directions even if he's never heard of Camden Town. Old soul. Tired from having come back repeatedly. No longer mindful of detail, just living out, yet again, the duties and obligations.'

They were out of breath, going up the slope. The Town

Hall was coming up on the right, the petrol pump on the left. 'The new souls?' asked Ananda. 'Oh, they're all around us,' said his uncle. 'There's a great impatience to be born.' Ananda felt a rustling, a single-minded urgency in the air. Dappled. 'The new souls are competing to be born and experience sensuous pleasures—bars, sex, cars, big homes. They want all that—soon.'

*

They reached the top, the head of the T, and turned left. They had, as yet, no plan. They appeared to be heading for Hampstead. It was hard to know who was following whose lead; neither wanted to consciously take the upper hand, although Ananda's uncle came up with impromptu suggestions: 'Let's cross, there's more shade on the other side', and 'Don't step on that, be careful. The English let their dogs defecate anywhere.' His uncle muttered imprecatory caveats if they approached a dog's stool. They went past the Trust House Forte hotel, and across the zebra crossing before a posh pub and the new KFC, coming to the church whose name they didn't know. Here they slowed down, catching their breath, but also in deference to the building. They couldn't recall having ever spotted activity around it. They presumed (without saying this aloud) it must be abandoned. In spite of the rest of the road being sunlit, the green around the church had a stubble of shadow darkening it, as if there were a cloud

They sat down at last at the base of the hill, in a homely-looking tea shop. Ananda's uncle tapped his sneakers. 'These are very comfortable. No matter how much you walk, your feet will never hurt in these.' They were grey and ugly. He eyed Ananda's brown leather shoes. 'You should change those,' he advised. 'You'll be much happier.' Picking up the menu, he protested: 'No rum baba!' Then read: 'Strudel, merring, fruit tart—*dhur*, the English have become too fancy of late.' There was a new internationalism afoot in London, and he bristled against it. 'You don't get treacle tart any more,' he said contemptuously. 'There are only a few pubs in London where you can get treacle tart.' His baritone was filling up the space by the window where they sat. A woman two tables away glanced swiftly back. After reflecting further on the fact that there seemed to be a recent recoil in the nation from extremities of sweetness, they ordered tea and a muffin. Ananda, by now, realised that his uncle was going to make no enquiry about how he was or what frame of mind he was in (despite knowing his nephew was unremittingly, even tediously, unhappy in Warren Street). He wasn't going to ask after his parents either.

So Ananda said anyway: 'Those people upstairs are always making a racket. They start at midnight. Telling them not to hasn't worked.' He stared at the cubes of sugar. 'Today's Friday, they'll be up later than usual.'

His uncle wasn't listening. Instead, he said to Ananda: 'Pupu, have you heard this song?'

Bhalobeshe jadi shukho nahi
Tabe keno eto bhalobasha?

If loving gives no happiness
Why do we love so much?

He'd begun to hum the lines, one elbow on the table. His eyes were droopy; semi-ecstatic. The woman at the nearby table was pretending not to hear. It was one of Tagore's limpest compositions. But if he said so, there might be a build-up to a scene. They had several of those over Tagore, or Ananda's mother, or this or that relation—the scenes had their cathartic uses, but were best averted. His uncle could become warlike about Tagore; so best to be peaceable. If Ananda answered with, 'No, I haven't heard it,' his uncle would say: '*What?* Your repertoire of songs is rather small.' Instead, Ananda said:

'I *have* heard it—from you. If you recall, you've been singing it each time we've met this month.'

Every time. His uncle must be in love. Either from a transient thrill of recognition, smiles exchanged between him and a shop girl, or unrequited devotions. Unrequited was not the appropriate word. For love not to be reciprocated, the object of the emotion must know they're loved. There was no knowledge here. It was in his uncle's head—as a tumultuous event. Shortly before he'd retired, his uncle had fallen in love with Gilberta, who used to help her mother with the odd janitorly chore at Philipp Bros. The office janitress was a

163

Portuguese woman called Rosa. Gilberta was a sixteen-year-old: a picture of innocence evidently—when his uncle wasn't tackling Freddy Gamble and Paul Middleton's leftover work, he studied her as she scrubbed the floor. He was stricken with melancholy; because he loved her, and believed that—if he'd had the courage, the temerity—she would have loved him.

'Do you know what she did once?' he'd said to Ananda during one of their several discussions about Gilberta, a faint look of horror on his face.

'What?'

'I could see her in front of the bathroom standing with mop and bucket (I was the one person at work, everyone had gone). I wasn't sure if she knew I was there. Next moment, she knelt in front of the bucket as if to wipe something, and—looking straight at me—gestured with her hand towards the place down there'—his own hand hovered fleetingly above his crotch: he was still a bit scandalised—as though an epiphany had turned out to be its opposite.

'What happened?'

'Nothing. What could happen? I pretended not to see. She finished and left.'

Ananda had then taken the opportunity to bring to light a question that had troubled him, though why he thought his uncle would know the answer wasn't clear—for some reason, he believed his uncle carried within him some intractable wisdom distilled by his asociability: so he'd put to him—'What's important to women—love or sex?'

'Sex,' his uncle had said, taking no special pleasure in the reply, just acknowledging a fact.

Both, heads bowed, had allowed a moment to pass as Ananda absorbed the impact of the news. For such plain-speaking, Ananda knew (from his background reading on *The Waste Land*) that Tiresias, who'd experienced what it meant to be both man and woman ('old man with wrinkled dugs'), had been struck blind by the vindictive Hera.

In his first year in London, Ananda had had to hear about Gilberta repeatedly. His uncle wasn't over her. He spoke at length, now praising her, now offering his summations and suspicions, weighing her gestures and the inadvertent eye-contact between them, the banter she engaged in with Paul Middleton. Much had passed over his heart. Ananda marvelled, and quietly fulminated, that his uncle should make so much out of so little. For his uncle and Gilberta hardly knew each other outside their inane day-to-day encounters. To her, he was another man in the office. Mr Nandy. Or maybe she didn't know his name. Why then was he moaning (to use the very English term his uncle used to put down Ananda with when he spoke plaintively of home)? Then again, how necessary was contact? Dante had met Beatrice twice. Not met—maybe just *seen*. A total of fifteen minutes . . . And what about Meera bai, who'd dumped her husband, the king, for her 'lord' and lover, the flute-playing Krishna? What of those songs and poems coming out of—not contact, let alone consummation, but wish-fulfilment and fantasy? Was it some sort of pathetic fallacy, to presume that lives were animated by love when they were actually quickened by the imagination? How many people were there today who loved quietly without hope of consummation: to whom conventional sexual fulfilment was unimportant? You might not be aware of them, but they probably wrote the love poems. (Larkin sprang to mind: curmudgeonly bachelor.)

Ananda wondered if his uncle was still susceptible to Gilberta. Why was he humming the maudlin tune?

'Really?' His uncle was stung at the implication that he'd been singing it too frequently. Ananda resented that his uncle often tried to subtly undermine him (dismissive as he was of modernism and slyly sceptical of Ananda's mission as a poet), but his uncle probably felt the same way about Ananda—that his nephew deflated him at crucial moments. He persisted: 'But what do you think of the song?'—for Tagore's reputation, on all fronts, must be jealously overseen.

'Maybe not quite my cup of tea,' said Ananda.

On cue, the waitress came with a pot of tea and cups and saucers on a tray, as well as the muffin his uncle had insisted on ordering for Ananda. 'Here we are,' she said (she was middle-class and cheerily aloof), 'Thank you!'; a stream of Thank yous followed—dutiful, upbeat, insincere, grateful—each time something was unloaded off the tray.

Both of them—but his uncle in particular—were feeling a bit out of place. It was clear that his uncle wished they were in one of those self-service tea shops. The sort with rum baba and trays on top of each other. His uncle didn't know how to whisper, and he said in Bengali: 'There are places I know where you can get a cup of tea and an excellent cheesecake for half the price.'

Did he not feel a sense of belonging any more in this area? Though his uncle used to despise his bhadralok contemporaries in Belsize Park, they'd at least *been* there, earlier, to despise and avoid. They were long vanished, to Stoke Newington or Pinner. Those people, fifteen years in the London boroughs, had grown-up children now, who—because their parents had saved on heating and electricity—had gone to the best private schools and were presently either at university or starting to look for jobs. Only his uncle had stayed on, in 'Hampstead', rejecting the suburbs and the married life and family that inevitably accompanied them—the Shah his interlocutor. Ananda sensed his uncle's grumbling ennui as he poured tea into the cup. From the pane on Ananda's right, they gazed at where the hill leading to the Heath descended and made a trough with the bottom of Pond Street, and, lit by the sun, displayed a junction with a zebra crossing and a bus stop.

'Pupu,' said his uncle, 'have the muffin.' His tone bordered on hectoring. 'It's very good,' he claimed, without having tasted it. 'We mustn't waste it.' That was the reason for the advocacy: it was an expensive muffin. Ananda resisted the urge to say, *I never wanted it*, and replied, 'You have it.' Because he knew this was why his uncle had ordered it—he was hungry. He hadn't had anything after all that sugar at breakfast. (Here, he'd only put four cubes in his cup and stirred it slowly.) His uncle said, '*Tumi khao*.' 'No, I won't, really—you go ahead,' said Ananda. His uncle regarded the muffin with dislike (for being undemocratically overpriced). Then he picked it up and took a huge mouthful, his eyelids drooping, his throat rippling, as he swallowed—till he could breathe again, and utter the verdict: 'Very good . . .' His whole body was curiously relaxed.

* * *

'Keats used to live here,' said his uncle.

Foxes, Glenda Jackson—and Keats. Hampstead. Rangamama too, in a manner of speaking. But was Belsize Park truly Hampstead?

'Mukherjee used to say to me—"*Moshai*, have you seen Keats's house?" I was never interested in Keats's house.' Confessed to matter-of-factly, as he devoured the muffin. Still, he mentioned Keats no doubt because his nephew was 'reading' English literature; although his equivocations and qualifications about this were a reminder coming from sideways about whether or not English literature was a subject worth studying. But Keats was useful to establishing the brilliance of this address—its ineffable pedigree. Mukherjee must be a bit of an English lit aficionado. A bachelor, and for two years Ananda's uncle's other neighbour in the basement. Ananda had never seen him. Yet he was always speaking to his uncle, this man, about facets of English culture.

'Hm,' said Ananda. His uncle always provided such a steady stream of opinion that he seldom felt like voicing his own: but he harboured views on everything.

Oddly, he wasn't touched by Keats. The poetry, that is. Maybe because he'd had to study 'Ode to a Nightingale' in school, and, precocious and ignorant, glutted himself on the young poet's over-rich vocabulary, on mouthfuls of phrases such as 'blushful Hippocrene'. Already a poet in his own eyes, Ananda, at fifteen, had judged Keats by the standards of his own subjectivity, and found him a little—bland. Keats was too perfect. Ananda had never recovered from that first encounter—poet to poet, young adult to young man. He looked semi-sensitively around him through the glass pane, to guess at where Keats might have been or still be. He'd written of summer only in passing, in the short-breathed 'Grasshopper and the Cricket'. Outside, the day was golden. Busy. The Odeon might have disappeared, but cars were going up all the time past the Royal Free Hospital. Ananda was unreceptive to the poetry—but he was moved by the man. He could see him, almost. Good-looking, terribly short. Possibly because of the early privations and illnesses. He did not grow. He did not grow old in a number of ways. A man-boy.

Ananda was in England because of Keats. He'd begun reading the letters around the time he was applying to colleges in London. He was won over: it was the first time he'd felt a writer's nearness, his heartbeat. When he was offered a place (in the college where he was now a student), they'd asked him to write a short account of his reading. He'd typed out a page and a half, of which the last quarter was devoted entirely to Keats's letters. Richard Bertram had told Ananda that he had it on good authority that it was this piece of writing—which they'd wanted from him in lieu of an interview—that had secured his admission. So Ananda was beholden to the twenty-six-year-old.

In that little document he'd sent to the college, he hadn't mentioned how affected he'd been by Keats's love for Fanny Brawne. A desire unfulfilled. At some point, it had dawned on

Keats that he'd never marry Fanny because he was dangerously ill. An insoluble conundrum—how to make a future with a person when you knew you were going to die? Ananda himself had experienced a prohibited love: for a cousin. When he was twenty, he was warned never to see her again. This was among the reasons for London being a place of exile. And why he must prove to himself that he'd have a future—as a poet—without her.

How real was Fanny Brawne to Keats? How much had he invented her (as Ananda knew he'd to an extent invented his cousin)? Was a beloved even necessary to experiencing love? Similarly, did you have to experience life to be a writer, or to have a subject at hand? These were two kinds of belief where an 'actual' experience seemed beside the point—of believing you were in love; and that you were a writer. Was Keats's short life as a poet essentially one of make-believe? Was he pretending, with a unique faith and intensity, that he was a poet? At least in 'Ode to Psyche', which Ananda liked, Keats had embraced the make-believe of being a priest for a goddess he knew didn't quite exist: 'Yes, I will be thy priest, and build a fane / In some untrodden region of my mind.'

'Rabi Thakur was in Hampstead,' his uncle said. The plate that had borne the muffin was spotless. He'd taken care of each crumb—from his continuing hunger, but also out of a moral obligation to do justice to a piece of food he'd spent money on. Less than a minute had passed since Keats was mentioned. Ananda didn't believe his uncle could survive much longer—once a poet's name came up—without talking about Tagore. For him, there was one poet only. He'd said as much. Maybe it was the appearance: the imposing height; the bearded, Olympian air; the bright disarming eyes. Also the delicacy and sophistication of the language ('He single-handedly changed Bengali').

And, in keeping with his subtly divine qualities, there was the fact that (as his uncle had explained): 'He created not only a great body of work but a generation. I wouldn't have been who I am were it not for Tagore. My father'—he hardly knew his father; he'd died when Radhesh was three in a riding accident, but he'd conjured him up thoroughly—'was a very different man from I. Because he belonged to the world before Tagore.'

Judiciously he added, studying Ananda, the English literature student: 'When you use a poet's name as an adjective—say, "Wordsworthian" or "Keatsian"—you mean the style he's well-known for. But when you say *Rabindrik* you don't just mean something literary, but a way of life, an ethos that shaped a generation. Can you say that of another poet?' End of speech. Leaving Ananda to mull over whether the reign of Rabi Thakur could be countered. Whether it was even important to a poet to 'create' a generation.

'What do you think he'd have made of you?'

'Me?'

'Yes—supposing you'd met.'

His uncle had bowed his hairless head and said, without

172

rancour, but passionately on Tagore's behalf: 'I don't think he would have been able to stand me.'

Ananda had seen the house. Uncle and nephew had, one day, made a detour from the Heath when they'd gone out walking. One of their pointless rambles. Suddenly, the round blue plaque: *INDIAN POET stayed here in 1912*. A lonely vigil. Not a passer-by in the lane—that wasn't unusual. Beautiful house, protected by a filigree of branches. Did his uncle know that Tagore's time was long gone? It would be too harsh to say out loud. If, as his uncle claimed, a generation had been minted and fashioned by the bearded one—including his parents and their voluble neighbours in Belsize Park— then to deny him was also to cast them into non-existence. Which, in a sense, was what had happened. Tagore was hardly remembered. And to be a Bengali in London meant being the owner of a Bangladeshi restaurant. What a joke, what a come-down! And if he *was* spoken of, it was with polite incomprehension—or mockery. Or, worse, with wide-eyed incomprehension by some Englishman who wasn't interested in poetry but in 'India'. Hilary Burton and Richard Bertram never mentioned him; Nestor Davidson had quizzically enquired after him—'What *do* you think of Tagore?'—as if he were an exotic annual ritual or an ailment. Deep in his heart, his uncle must know.

'Could we have the bill please?' Ananda murmured to the waitress as she passed. The English hadn't been made for serving but for nannying, to remind you punctiliously to cross your t's; most people who served were foreigners—it started with the army of tenacious Sikh women with mops and pails who hovered around you, like a wedding party, when you got into Heathrow. 'Of course!' she sang out.

'Pupu,' his uncle warned, 'this one's on me.' He had a look, as if anticipating rebellion. It was all show. His uncle would pay—they both knew that. Yet his uncompromising air allowed Ananda to feel the glow of love—an avuncular love that was never not slightly comical (so poorly was Rangamama, despite his reputation for past glory, cut out to be mentor). Ananda thought he'd slip in a word again about apprehensions brewing at the back of his mind:

'There's sure to be trouble tonight. They sleep late on Fridays.'

'It's one of the ways you can tell an alien from a human being. People who live among us, look like us, but come from elsewhere,' said his uncle. 'Aliens sleep when ordinary people wake—they wake when others sleep. If you observe this oddity in someone's habit, you should keep in mind that they may not be from here.'

This did fit in with the Patels' and even Mandy's sleep patterns. When his uncle expounded these theories, he didn't always let on about his sources. They might be something he'd taken note of years ago in Sylhet; or from his reserves of the *Pan Book of Horror Stories*; or from a piece of research about the supernatural and the afterlife—which his family had been interested in since he was a child.

They'd tried out the planchette in Sylhet—a kind of seance. The pencil went crazy, wrote by itself, impelled by a spirit. This pencil gave one- or two-word bulletins; cryptic declarations. Most of the message was lost, as with a wireless which, despite you rolling the knobs or shifting its position, couldn't capture the signal. The technology connecting the here to the hereafter was still imperfect. Perhaps it was the early death of the father, in 1926, which had left the family rudderless, that led them—especially Radhesh's older brothers and older sister—to take up this pursuit. Or maybe it also involved a genuine curiosity about the migration of souls. They'd made contact with an English schoolteacher, dead of typhoid, who'd spelt out the nonsensical remark, *Met him Sykes hoses.* However, they were mostly able to find one who gave them news of the spiritual progress of people they'd known—celebrated as well as local and familial figures. Ananda's uncle had told him the seventh stage was the highest a soul could ascend to. 'Amalesh Tripathi, a businessman and philanthropist in Sylhet, was in the *second* stage—despite all his charitable work,' said his uncle. There was a glimmer of satisfaction in his eye. 'Wonder why.' Proudly he'd told Ananda: 'Our father was in the fourth stage. Very good'—as of a favourite bright child who'd, as expected, shone at an exam. Finally, the big news, in a quiet, vindicated tone: 'Tagore was in the sixth stage.' They would have been told this by a spirit in the 1940s, no doubt (Tagore had died in 1941), in Shillong, where the family moved prior to Partition, still rudderless.

'I sleep poorly myself,' pointed out Ananda as they awaited the bill. 'Could it mean I'm from another planet?'

'Whatever you do,' said his uncle firmly, 'don't drink milk before you go to bed because people have told you that it's a cure for insomnia. You'll feel bloated. We had an aunt who had a fixation about milk—as a result my growing up and even my youth was a purgatory. I gave up milk a few years after coming to London. Since then my life has been a life of freedom.'

*

A moment later, staring out of the window, distracted, he said, '*Pupu, mone chhata pore achhe.*' Ananda hadn't ever heard anyone else use this expression. It was something you'd expect an old village woman to say. Literally, it meant, 'There's a covering of moss on my heart.' He was vaguely sad—why, on this bright day, it was hard to tell. He never owned up to homesickness—though he'd lived in 24 Belsize Park for twenty-six years now. He said he was happy; his only cause of distress his rejection of the directorship. When Ananda complained of missing home, he showed little sympathy. Yet, sometimes during a walk, or in the middle of a walk, he'd say: 'Mone chhata pore achhe.'

'Why, what's the matter?' Did his mother leaving last week have anything to do with it? 'Ma was asking after you yesterday.'

'Tell her not to spend your father's money on long-distance

calls. She lives on some other plane, your mother. Thinks she's Queen Elizabeth!' Still resentful she wasn't hanging around for him. Khuku, the sidekick; envying her her posh married life in Bombay. And maybe missing her?

Ananda bristled. Yet he held back from leaping into the fray. On one of his mother's recent visits, when she'd come to London to allay Ananda's restiveness, Rangamama had attacked her physically, rudely yanking her hair when she'd dared to defend the older brother in Shillong whom Ananda's uncle was sounding off about for repeatedly demanding money from him. Instinctively, Ananda had shoved him, and, to his surprise, sent him reeling, realising how lightly built his uncle was, a wisp of a man.

'Calls herself an artist!' he continued, undaunted. He was now taunting her for what he perceived to be her hubris as a singer. All her childhood she'd been enshrined within her family for her singing voice. Ten days ago, she'd excused her inability to understand complex financial arrangements by saying (not without levity) to the world—actually, to the room in Warren Street—that after all she was an 'artist'. 'Artist!' said his uncle. 'She doesn't know what an arse is, let alone art!'

'She *is* an artist,' insisted Ananda. 'Her voice is amazing. It's your family's fault—not sending her to Santiniketan—or to college for that matter. Disgraceful!'

'You're right,' conceded his uncle. 'That was a bad mistake. The family was completely out of money at the time. But if *I* had been responsible, she'd have finished her education.'

Pronounced grandiosely, but with passion. 'And Satish married her because of *me*. I extracted that promise from him.'

'And it's because of *her*,' said Ananda, 'that you two good-for-nothings are where you are today—one a managing director and the other a would-be director with a giant-size pension. Because she worked in the naval department at Aldwych while you two ate her cooking and sat your exams.'

'Rubbish—that's not true.' A transient malevolent smile passed over his face. Was he toying with him?

'Did you not,' persisted Ananda, 'live off her earnings in 24 Belsize Park?'

A swift assessment of evidence. Penitently he replied: 'I've never denied it. I've never denied what she did for me. Or that I am what I am because of her.'

'There you are! Thank you!' A piece of paper on a plate, so precarious it might blow away any second. The waitress had vanished almost as soon as she'd placed it on the table.

'Wait, let me get this.' He lifted a restraining palm. From the inside breast pocket he took out, with grace and regret, a carefully tucked-in wad of pound notes. He plucked a five-pound note from the inner whorl and laid it on the plate. Ananda almost felt sorry for him, so immersed he was, so *alone* too, and clearly had been. Ananda was beholden. He couldn't have afforded this tea shop. It was 'dear'; the bill had come to three pounds ten. 'How much?' he asked. 'Nothing,' his uncle said mysteriously, as if he were hiding an embarrassing sexual secret from an innocent—but Ananda had bent forward and read the scrawled figure. The waitress turned up again by magic; 'Thank you!'—now she'd borne the plate with the five-pound note aloft. His uncle had given her a dazzling smile, as if she were an angel they'd been lucky to have watch over them. He displayed the gap where his front incisor was until a year ago. Dental work was too costly in Britain. He'd go to India and get it fixed. It was a plan. Till then, he'd brandish the gap.

He'd lost the tooth in an idiotic episode. He was returning late on one of his nocturnal sojourns, via a lonely stretch on Chalk Farm, when he'd had the core of a recently consumed apple flung at him by a skinhead who was sitting on a low wall with two friends. As a rule, his uncle avoided making eye-contact with skinheads, because it was unsettling to look at a visage that had no facial hair. Like looking at a face that was all eye: a giant angry eye. But something possessed his uncle to go to the one who'd thrown the core and say: 'Why did you do that?' It was well past the heyday of skinheads, so this one merely punched him, rather than kill him, as he would have when the National Front was in season. Somewhere in Chalk Farm, a mile and a half from where they were now, his uncle had lost a tooth.

*

The change, back on the table—a squat pound coin and nine pieces of what could have been silver. 'Sorry for the wait!

Thank you!' The endless metronome-like swing between apologies and expressions of gratitude. In the song, 'In a daily dance / in my consciousness / who dances / ta ta thai thai', the dancer's arc moved from infinity on the one foot to finitude on the other; from bereavement to laughter. Here, in London, Sorrys and Thank yous covered the day in the same dance, in an ever-repeating back-and-forth.

'How much should we leave her?' Ananda's uncle's face was grim. Tipping was occasion for exaggerated theatre.

'Thirty—maybe forty at most.'

'Should I leave a pound? A pound would look nice. She *has* been friendly.'

'A pound!' Ananda was exasperated by his uncle's indiscriminate sense of justice. What made him moan non-stop about sending cheques to his brother in Shillong, but be so cavalier with his money to a stranger? 'You can't possibly leave a pound!'

'She must be quite poor,' substituting the fact that he had no basis for the statement with an annoying look of maternal compassion—as if he were speaking of some down-at-heel cousin or beggar-maid he'd known in his childhood.

'*Thank* you sir!' said the waitress when she spotted her reward, a bit shocked. She probably felt she'd taken advantage of this poor demented man, clearly unfamiliar with English currency.

He ducked his head. 'It was a jolly good tea, you know!' he lied.

They emerged from the hut-like space. These rural log-cabins were expensive; the tea shops with modern furniture and fittings were common: the paradox of Hampstead. Except there were no common tea shops here.

* * *

'Well?'

'What?'

'Bus or tube?'

A dilemma on the pavement before the tea shop. They contemplated the bus stop at South End Green. Not because they intended to go somewhere—but simply because, as his uncle had once said, 'You can see more from a bus.' A couple of months ago, he, his uncle, and his mother had got on to a bus destined to travel in an exploratory circle and bring them back to where they'd begun, the South End Green terminus. It had been a week of frayed nerves; Ananda was struggling with *Paradise Lost* and Milton justifying the ways of God to men as, above him, the Patels erupted without warning into movement and rap music. But the bus ride had lifted them, literally (since they decided to sit on the upper deck). They'd floated—if not over London, then over its streets, encountering, at eye-level, a succession of treetops and half-open first-storey windows. When Ananda had remarked, taking in the illuminated residential vistas, 'I'll need to get back to the Milton essay tonight—exams start in three weeks,' his uncle, with a scandalised gasp (from the horror of past exams taken and half-remembered), said, 'You're lucky to be calm. When there's work before me, I can never take pleasure in things till it's out of the way.' Of course, his uncle had no work before him—he'd presumably need to invent some to feel again the true sensation of pleasure.

Now they could cross and board the stationary 517, or walk past Keats's house and, near the Heath, take the A11.

'No let's go to Belsize Park.' The final decision, when he chose to exercise it, was Ananda's.

'Take the tube?'

'Yes—to King's Cross.'

Why to a stop as uninviting as King's Cross wasn't clear. Yet his uncle nodded, as if he'd been given counsel full of wisdom.

They went back up Pond Street, skirting the Royal Free Hospital.

'Sing that one Pupu: *se din dujane dulechhinu boney*'—one of Rabi Thakur's commonest ditties, common but lovely.

'Not now.'

Ananda was humming a raga: Purvi. His uncle couldn't abide classical music. Not only because of its demonstrative virtuosity, which he regarded with contempt. (Anything outside his ken was beneath him. He bowed to no superior form or authority.) But also the sacred context of classical music embarrassed him. Being a Tagorean, he saw the universe in a bright humanist radiance. Any mention in songs of Hari, Radha, or Ram made him flinch. That's what the Brahmo antecedents of modern Bengal had done—turned the Bengali into a solitary voyager, with no religion and nothing but a raiment of poems, Tagore songs, and—instead of deities—novelists and poets.

Ananda stubbornly sang Purvi going up to Haverstock

Hill. A car crept up on a zebra crossing. No one blew the horn here. Ananda preferred to practise twice a day. On some days he gave his voice a holiday. He managed this routine because of his peculiar relationship with the university. His tutors, certainly Mr Davidson, had given him a cautious berth—lecturers barely noticed him and his absences. Since he'd forgone a second spell of practice today, he felt a pang of remorse. Saraswati, whom he looked up to, might notice. Nubile, private, plucking on the veena—from her remote domain reigning over the arts.

'Pupu—*se din dujane!*'

Finally Ananda surrendered.

That day when we together
Were suspended in the forest
On a swing that was threaded with flowers.

They were in front of the church; the neighbouring school was closed, or there would have been children rushing past. Ananda hesitated to sing in Warren Street for fear of being overheard. In the streets, he felt less constrained. His uncle, his eyes closed in emotion and pain, was so absorbed he didn't notice people walking by. He might be indifferent to Ananda's future as a modernist poet and only cursorily concerned with his progress as a student—but he adored the way he sang Tagore. If he'd had his way (in a utopia, his uncle would have been an autocrat), he'd have had Ananda give up writing and every loyalty to classical music, and only perform Tagore songs. So it was just as well his word wasn't law.

May that small memory
Awaken in your mind
From time to time—don't forget it.

'Beautiful!' Eyes three quarters closed; Ananda could glimpse the whites through the slits. Somehow they made their way to Haverstock Hill.

'This song brings back a beautiful memory—but full of sadness.'

'Really?'

'Yes. It was in Sylhet. In a garden in the evening. A girl I knew was nearby. There was something in the air. But, ah! I couldn't tell her my feelings.'

It was the first Ananda had heard of this. Because no object of affection had been referred to prior to Gilberta.

'I knew I'd never tell her.'

'Was it someone you had a relationship with?'

'No, no.' The term 'relationship' was anachronistic; it didn't make sense here. But Ananda was thinking of his non-adventure with his cousin.

'Did you have sex with her?' Another misguided query. Ananda knew this the moment he spoke: Rangamama was a virgin, wasn't he?

*

'The weather feels like Shillong.'

Yes, the air outside the church had been reminiscent. Ananda remembered, from visits to extended family a decade ago, the hill station's dry summer sun.

Not turning left at once towards the tube station, they crossed to the Trust House Forte Hotel—*then* turned. They were physically in the realm of Ananda's 1973 visit: the meeting over curry with the Shah; unwieldy kippers at the hotel's breakfast buffet; Cliff Richard and the Bee Gees; his uncle with sideburns dropping past his ears, his skull still not quite visible, as it was now. Ananda felt distant from that visit though he was in its vicinity; even the bar and smoking room of the hotel, seen through the large windows, looked unrecognisable—their arrangements altered.

'Did you ever write poetry yourself?'

Ananda put it to his uncle not to challenge him but because it seemed a worthwhile query. Not least because his uncle was such a dogmatic propagandist for Rabi Thakur, who he routinely said was 'the greatest lyric poet ever'. A 'lyric *kobi*', in his uncle's vocabulary, was superior to every other variable of poet—a magical being, sighted hardly ever, like the fox or the badger. 'The life of a lyric kobi is very brief,' his uncle had informed Ananda, who had no idea if the statement were a literal or figurative one. Ananda knew that many young men in Sylhet wrote poetry. His own father Satish—for long a man of commerce and finance—had been among them. Ananda's mother had told her son that Satish was well known, when he was seventeen, for writing short and sad poems that ended in ellipses. The poems must have been about love because those who'd read them referred to the ellipses as '*asrur phota*' or 'teardrops'.

'I left that sort of thing to others,' said his uncle as, looking right and left, they walked past Belsize Avenue. 'It's possible to take shortcuts writing poetry in English. There are no shortcuts to writing Bengali poetry.'

So not only was he claiming to be different from deluded friends (including Ananda's father) who had, seized by the poetry bug, fooled themselves into thinking they were poets: he was having a go at Ananda and the new species he belonged to, of aberrants who'd elected to write, ridiculously, in English. Shortcuts! Was he saying that it was easier to be a fraudulent poet in English than in Bengali?

'Of course Chhorda began by writing some remarkable poems.' This was the older brother in Shillong. That he'd grown partly dependent on his younger brother since retiring from the state civil service led Radhesh to feel a vicious recoil against a man he'd once worshipped for his refinement and even been intimidated by. 'He asks me for money now, he used to treat me like an errand boy then!' A couple of times in Warren Street he'd even called Chhorda sneeringly by his pet name—Manu. Which had provoked Ananda's mother to heartfelt protest and remonstrance. Which had led to his uncle tugging her by the hair in rage and Ananda giving *him* a push that sent him flying back. They came to the steps of the Hampstead Town Hall, his uncle adding proudly: 'What a sensation it was when *Desh* published one of his poems when he was sixteen!' It was a big deal to have a poem out in *Desh* in those days, whether you were from Calcutta or Sylhet, sixteen or sixty.

'Was it good? The poem?' Ananda was well aware that his uncle had it by heart.

'It was beautiful—yes.' He made the inevitable qualification: 'Naturally, it bore the imprint of Tagore's diction and cadence. Very hard to escape that.' English poets couldn't match Tagore for his finesse. European poets largely didn't exist. And no Bengali poet, whether it was his older brother or the great Jibanananda Das, could avoid visiting a tone and terrain that was already Tagore's. Better, then, for the Bengali not to write poetry at all, and just read Tagore; his uncle had demonstrated the wisdom of this in the decision he'd long ago taken: to abstain.

'Also, that first flush—when Chhorda saw the world in a peculiar vibrant glow, in a colour close to purple—that faded. He told me he could never see that vivid colour after seventeen. Then he stopped writing poems.' And became a minor addition to the Assam Civil Service.

*

They paused before the Screen on the Hill. There was nothing to draw them immediately. Mostly the Screen on the Hill catered to the delicate art-house audience that lived in this environment. Contrary, lonely English people who were at once deeply, visibly English and gently Francophile. Hardly any of the movies that he and his uncle liked to watch together—James Bond played by Sean Connery. Tonight at 7 p.m. it was *Discreet Charm of the Bourgeoisie*.

*

Ananda's uncle's older brother's poem. From *Desh*. He'd recited it during one of their strolls round the area, as if it were a canonical event, something that had subtly changed the world—at least his world. It was a strange poem for a sixteen-year-old to write—neither idealistic nor excessively emotional, but one that quietly observed a small but decisive transition in the young poet's life. At first, Ananda thought it was addressed, as is the norm, to a woman—perhaps real, but probably imaginary. Then he heard from his uncle that these were lines written by his brother to their late father. Like 'Surprised by Joy', which records the realisation, in the midst of the poet's natural elation, of the fact of his dead daughter's absence, his uncle's poem—the uncle who lived in Shillong— acknowledged the memory (breaking the day's everyday, forgetful rhythm) that his father was gone; yet not quite gone. Written years ago. What did it mean to grow up without a father? Ananda knew that his grandfather was an engineer, and that his death in the riding accident had left his wife and

189

children struggling. They'd never recovered. Ananda's mother had been two when her father died; Rangamama three and a half. He'd maybe taken it worse than the others—it gave him an exaggerated sense of what he might have been. The older siblings had rallied, but for a while dabbled in the planchette to establish their father's whereabouts. Then they'd set aside that nonsense in favour of marrying and having children, for the relief of letting their own childhood go.

*

'I wasn't cut out for writing poems. Didn't have the time for that kind of thing,' said his uncle with manly pride. 'I had to be there—have to be there—for my family. I chose that role for myself.'

The black sheep, ordered to run errands. Used-car salesman. Now living in the cave in 24 Belsize Park, issuing cheques to a list of petitioners—close as well as obscure relations (relations' relations) whom Ananda had never heard of—in corners of Bengal and Assam. The solitary, faraway pillar of a family scattered and dispersed: that's how his uncle saw himself.

They were near the Belsize Bookshop. Its half-forgotten cocoon always a temptation to encroach on. To his uncle he said:

'You don't *have* to write poems. There are people who make their *life* a poetic work. You may be one of them.'

Rangamama didn't so much accompany his nephew as

skulk slightly behind. Sometimes, when they were shoulder to shoulder, they collided sideways. His uncle nodded. He seemed intrigued. Certainly, the analysis was in tune with his own self-mythologising. (Having absorbed Ananda's words, he would probably quote them back to him three days later, imagining he'd thought them up himself.) Once, in the course of a heated dialogue in which his uncle's greatness was clearly not being adequately addressed, he'd snapped: 'Do you realise I'm God?' Instead of pointing him to a psychiatrist, Ananda had controlled himself and replied that maybe all men, in some capacity, were God, and they'd both had the good sense to leave it at that. Another time, when they were discussing Ananda's father's many attractive qualities, his composure and general sanity, his uncle had said competitively: 'There are many planes of existence. The people on the lower don't see the ones on the higher. For example, there are beings around us *now* we can't see. *Your* father can't really *see* me. I'm on a different plane—invisible to him, like a ghost.' Ananda had forgotten to throttle him because he was mesmerised. Another time: 'Do you know Jagannath?' The Lord of the Universe; yes, of course. 'Do you know why he's so ugly?' The likenesses of Jagannath were aboriginal, autochthonic: two stumps for arms; orbs for eyes—owl-like. 'As Jagannath created the universe, he gave more and more of himself, denuding his form—until he became what you see today: incredibly ugly; a misshapen stub.' Narrated with melodramatic quietude. When he searched for this version of the myth in books,

191

speaking in the poem? He'd been banished, hadn't he, for an obscure misdemeanour? By some Emperor? Was it Augustus? No, it couldn't be—Augustus was the guy after whom August was named. Would Ovid have been able to be so equanimous about the Nazis? Perhaps, in Tomis, on his sequestered estate, he wouldn't have heard too much about Auschwitz, except as rumour. Who were the 'damned' here? (Hindu theology had no concept of damnation—this could be why Ananda was fascinated by it.) Were they the wretched in the concentration camps? Or the functionaries and commanders who directed their fate? If the latter, then it was probably okay to make that ironical, faux mystical remark about them 'harmonizing strangely' with 'the divine love'. But if it was the former, then wasn't such a statement inadmissible, even revolting? He reconsidered the lines. For some reason, he found he'd been reading them each time as 'I have learned one thing: not to look down / Too much upon the damned'; rather than 'so much', as in the poem. He'd grown attached to the misreading. He smiled. It brought to the voice a senatorial wryness, the private sense of humour of a marginalised man. 'So much' gave Ovid an aloofness he couldn't possibly have had any more in Tomis.

Ananda put the *Collected Poems* where it had been, half leaning, half standing. He walked over to the Crime/ Horror section, where his uncle stood with his back to him, fussily poring over some pages as if they contained a legal correspondence. To see him doing anything silently was exemplary; he spoke incessantly, so that silence changed him, like those aliens he'd sometimes describe—those who are near us, deceptively normal.

'Which one?' Ananda asked, and his uncle blinked, smiling with genial remoteness.

It was *Skeleton Crew*—the new collection by Stephen King.

'Any good?' Ananda asked the question academically, without seriousness.

'It *is* good,' said his uncle. 'His stories are usually engrossing—about uncanny occurrences that change people's lives.' Approbation for a writer was unexpected, except where Tagore was concerned—out of tune with his personality.

The taste for Stephen King had evolved quite recently though, and swiftly. Ananda was still getting accustomed to it—to the unrelenting onward stride, after more than a decade defined by the *Pan Book of Horror Stories*.

'Maybe I should buy it,' said his uncle, narrowing his eyes. 'I've gone through all the books in the library.' By 'all' he meant horror, the supernatural, life after death—that queasy, uneasy addendum to literature; even so, it was unlikely he could have actually exhausted the lot. 'One of the staff said they're closing the library next year,' he added. Ananda was a bit taken aback. He'd never seen this library—never needed to—but hadn't thought it would just vanish. He read about such developments in the papers only with the faintest attention, events on the hazy outskirts of the endless, ugly debate about the National Health Service. Opera house closures. Local authorities. Public money. What would his uncle do now?

'Should I get it?' he said with agonised self-absorption. The question wasn't meant for Ananda; he was asking it of himself, aloud.

Ananda, eavesdropping, volunteered: 'If you need it, take it.' Horror, murder, like poetry, were addictions; they were meant to numb and enchant simultaneously—to insidiously engender the desire they satisfied. It depended on how much you could get by with—or without—in a day.

'I have one I'm midway through,' said his uncle, visibly doing some mental arithmetic. 'It should last me three—no, maybe four—days.' He was looking for reassurance about his chances of survival.

'Then you'll be fine,' said Ananda, trying desperately to extricate *Skeleton Crew* from his uncle's grip. 'You're in no desperate rush to get it.'

* * *

5

Heading for Town

The revellers headed for Leicester Square and Oxford Circus would increase in an hour.

Ananda plunged his hand into his pocket to take out the travel card valid till midnight. His uncle carried, in a flap in his wallet, his pensioner's travel pass, which gave him infinite freedom to avail himself of both spheres of London public transport—underworld and overground.

The shorn head on the pass was strangely futuristic.

'Never get your photo taken in a booth,' said his uncle. 'You'll look darker than you really are. It's because the booth cameras are adjusted to make white skin look normal.'

On descending, they were greeted by 'Morden via King's Cross 5 mins': a relief. On the tube, his uncle pointed out, 'Pupu—we could have seen a film.' But they had—last week. Ananda's mother had flown away, and they, returning from Heathrow to a London that seemed dream-like, had gone to the cinema. In the Leicester Square Odeon, their bodies clenching with each explosion and blow, they watched *A View to a Kill*. It was an irony that they both adored Sean Connery but had never watched him in a cinema in unison. The first Bond film they'd seen together—also Ananda's first Bond movie ever—was a Roger Moore, *Live and Let Die*. They'd caught it in Swiss Cottage in 1973. Last week, witnessing again with concern Roger Moore get into all sorts of scrapes but surviving them to brush the dust off his jacket and straighten his tie, Ananda's uncle had leaned towards him and murmured: 'Pupu, what would *we* do in such a situation? We'd be hopeless!' Despite Ananda's uncle setting up a somewhat presumptuous equivalence between them, it was true. They weren't designed for action. Actually, neither was good with even ordinary mechanical things. Ananda was sure this was why his uncle shunned the debit card. The most complex operation Ananda himself had completed was changing a light bulb (in his studio flat, but also for Mandy). Ananda wasn't sure if his uncle's ineptitude had anything to do with Saturn. 'Shani'—Saturn—'rules my life,' his uncle had told him, to account for the lack of momentum in his professional career. Ananda had read that people governed by Saturn were, besides being ditherers, great fumblers.

* * *

King's Cross was a paradoxical place at 6 p.m.: swarming with commuters, and lonely. Ignoring the rush, a bunch of people seemed to stand outside the station just waiting, smoking, kissing, or staring at the Pentonville Road.

'What are we doing here?' asked Ananda, raising his eyebrows.

'But it was very interesting when we came last!'

That was in the autumn, when the Durga Pujas were exiled from Hampstead to the Camden Town Hall—which was just out of sight of King's Cross Station. Harrumphing Bengalis with their slow-footed wives had suddenly appeared. They too—Ananda's mother, his uncle, he—had come, having heard of the move. They'd crossed at the traffic lights, not certain where, in the by-lanes, the venue was. His mother wasn't capable of long walks. It was Saptami, which, despite its meaning—'the seventh day'—was the start of festivities.

*

'Hello love, how are you?' A tall ungainly woman in a top revealing round white shoulders had been passing up and down, preoccupied, a cigarette in her cupped palm. Suddenly friendly with his uncle. Who seemed neither interested nor harried; he whispered to Ananda in that candid baritone: 'Be careful, there are many of them here.' Ananda felt affronted she hadn't addressed him. She'd looked through Ananda. What made his uncle worthy of the approach? He wondered what the rate was.

Difficult, this evening (it was getting on to half past six) to feel that Puja magic or, for that matter, the atmosphere of 'Dickens's London'. Turning into York Way, they found it hard to proceed. The pavement was thick with office workers waiting for buses.

They turned back to the station. The woman in the black top still hadn't found a man; she'd forgotten them, and hovered before the main entrance, purposeful and preoccupied.

'Let's go,' said Ananda.

'Yes, we can walk to Euston—to Ambala Sweets,' said his uncle.

'To Ambala Sweets now?'

'Yes, to get a few things. Their samosas are tremendous.'

But Ananda wasn't passionate about samosas. As for sweets—he hadn't inherited the overpowering sweet tooth gene from his uncle or his mother. In fact, Indian sweets in England invariably disappointed him—they had a vital ingredient missing: it might well be the ghee that lacked flavour. He knew what lay behind the plan. His uncle was gearing up to visit Warren Street—and he couldn't return (every visit to the studio flat, given it was occupied by family, by Ananda and sometimes Khuku, was for his uncle a homecoming) except bearing gifts. Even when he was a young man (Khuku had told Ananda), he was repeatedly, almost inadvertently, generous, and never came back to Sylhet from a trip without a sari. She used to be touched by this to the core because apparently there was no one else in the family aware that she'd become a young woman. That's why, now, in London—in spite of the fights they had—she'd forget his idiotic insults with infuriating rapidity.

The reason he came loaded with gifts was complicated. When Ananda came to London with his parents in 1983 to start at university, his uncle was in his 'I'm a no-good vagabond; Satish is the managing director' mode; so, whenever they ate out in the first two weeks of term, *there* would be Radhesh, tagging along as he did in the fifties, when he was impecunious and a satellite of the two. Freeloading daily into the small reserves of pounds sterling Ananda's father had kept aside for his son's upkeep. Unable to confront her brother, Khuku had confided in Basanta, a family friend who lived in Pinner. 'What do we do with Dada?' Basanta breached the confidence and had a word with Radhesh. So Radhesh reached Warren Street that evening fuming, carrying two bags of groceries. 'You think *I* want your company?' he'd said to his shocked audience. 'I don't need you at all! I visit you because *you* need *my* company.'

With some firefighting, that episode needed no further mentioning. But his uncle mostly visited carrying something. Usually stuff he'd long wanted to eat and hadn't had a chance to and would once he was hungry. Or even a packet of chicken liver he'd encourage Khuku to cook at once. Or, in her absence, samosas. Too many of them.

*

They went down the Euston Road—one of those stretches that was made for neither man nor animal, just the passing car. If there had been a spell of rain, it would have felt doubly inhospitable, but even on a summer's day that showed no sign of ending the road wasn't welcoming.

'Spare change please.'

Norman Tebbit's father: never did he presumably beg. He got on his bike and scoured the town for work. Luckily he didn't lose the bike, like the man in the Italian movie. This young man now, absorbing the sunshine, had thrown his words out on an off-chance. He wasn't terribly interested in the response. His uncle stopped, saying: 'One minute.' He turned, and, with slow strides, wove back. Stooping, he gave the man something. Shuffling back unhurriedly, he rejoined Ananda.

'How much?'

'Sorry?'

'How much did you give?' asked Ananda, as to a delinquent who erred recurrently.

'Oh nothing.' He ducked his head slightly. 'A pound'.

Ananda shook his head in resignation.

Yet his uncle looked put out; annoyed, even.

'He didn't say anything. Not even a Thank You. There was a time when beggars said God bless.'

So that's what it was! Too bad. But hadn't Jesus said (for his uncle admired and even identified with him; he'd once revealed to Ananda, at once tongue-in-cheek and completely without irony, 'I am Jesus Christ')—hadn't he said, 'When you give to the needy, do not let your left hand know what your right hand is doing, so that your giving may be in secret. And your Father who sees in secret will reward you'? When Ananda had read this, he'd thought of his uncle—how he hungered deeply for his virtues to be recognised, and how too he led a life indifferent to approbation. Ananda had also been impressed by Jesus's clarity. Christ was more than a populist preacher of love. That was clear from the retort: 'Render unto Caesar'—or was it Thatcher—'the things that are Caesar's, and unto God the things that are God's.'

But wasn't his uncle human and shrewd, and wouldn't his left hand be entitled to a degree of awareness of what the right hand was up to? Wasn't it expected—especially in one so solitary—that he might be often assigning value to his own actions? Who knows—maybe it wasn't enough for him for God alone to know of his small acts of empathy.

*

Past Euston Station they were, without much forewarning, at the sweet shop entrance; inside, a bunch of Indians flocked at the counter, abiding by no queue. The room held a strong suggestion of *kesar*.

On the tray in Rangamama's line of vision, flanked by neat diamond-shaped stacks of barfi on the left and some member of the great gulab jamun family on the right, and above another tray on the lower tier of pallid attempts at Bombay halwa, were exorbitant saffron-coloured laddoos. Motichur ladoo, a label said. My ass, thought Ananda. From Wembley, most likely.

'Pupu, look at those magnificent laddoos! *Durdanto*!'

Ananda had an inkling of doom that these were now destined to come his way, to be added to his kitchen paraphernalia.

'Should we get some of these?'

Since they were, in theory, intended for him, Ananda felt free to half-heartedly fend them off. 'Don't. They're fakes. They'll be nothing like the original.' It was the tragedy of London—to eat Indian food outside of the 'curry' and to constantly discover the unfamiliar in the familiar: dosas that looked like but didn't taste like dosas, bhelpuri that resembled bhelpuri but was something else. Not that he cared for the mythology of the laddoo. He had no idea why they were distributed jubilantly at North Indian celebrations. They were more a metaphor, a conceit, rather than a viable sweet. Their prestige had no explanation.

'Pupu *he*, I think you're wrong—I think we should try them. We have gulab jamun all the time.' He wanted them.

He'd probably never tasted a real laddoo in his life. After all, he'd never been to Delhi or Lucknow—he'd come to London straight after his youth in Shillong. He looked on with contained longing as six were arranged in a box: over-rich, oily orbs, flecked with pistachio. From his jacket pocket he took out an exactly folded Budgens bag and slipped the box in. He slid the bag across a wrist. Hand gloved in his right-hand pocket, the bag swinging imperceptibly, they made for Warren Street.

* * *

Ananda's mind went back to the woman circling around King's Cross. How many 'jobs' did she do in a day? Where? Or maybe his uncle was wrong—maybe she wasn't that kind of a woman. He'd once seen someone like her in front of Warren Street tube station: tall, with an overlarge body being shown off via a shoulderless top and mini skirt. Dressed like that in November. Ananda had noted her confused and visible air of incongruousness and expectancy; he'd glanced again, and (in the course of the second look) her unique calling had dawned on him. Instantly he'd thought, *I could be wrong. She might be waiting for a friend.* Anyway, he'd found neither her nor, today, the King's Cross woman interesting. He'd have to make a major effort of the imagination to want them. Moreover, he suspected that they might, by now, loathe sex. The brisk businesslike indifference that followed soon after the initial flirtatiousness of the two women in Bombay had swamped any confidence he might have had in the performance. Besides, he was terrified of this cruelly misnamed virus. It was largely exclusive to heroin-injectors and homosexuals, but 'largely' was the operative word. It had placed the King's Cross woman and her ilk forever out of bounds.

His uncle said AIDS was a myth. Western scaremongering. 'These kinds of diseases have been around forever. I saw people dying in Sylhet—of sexual deviancy. They've put a fancy name to it.'

Ananda had wondered about his uncle's abstinence. He'd considered the matter of his sexuality. In fact, at seventeen,

Ananda had even put the question to himself: *Could I be a homosexual?* He'd been worried—he didn't feel the sort of aggressive sexual desire towards girls he liked that he thought was appropriate. For two months, when he was seventeen, he'd tortured himself. Just as Sylvia Plath had confessed, 'I've begun to think like a Jew, feel like a Jew', he'd worked himself up to a state where he'd begun to feel and think like a gay person. But he found he could cope with this new identity. In the abortive business with the cousin, he'd invoked celebrated allies from history who'd purportedly fallen in love with theirs—Gautama Buddha, Atul Prasad, Satyajit Ray. And, in his agonised period, he summoned names to prove that creative people *had* to be gay: Ginsberg, Proust, Shakespeare. Then it occurred to him that he'd never wanted to kiss a man. The thought had no appeal at all. Soon, the notion that had gripped him melted, like a fever that had run its course. He went to the two prostitutes in order to confirm his sexuality. The matter was more or less settled.

It was settled where his uncle was concerned too. Ananda had looked for homoerotic inclinations, and found none. Could he be impotent? Ananda had said bluntly: 'Do you have wet dreams? You know what I mean?' His uncle had said, unflappable: 'I'm quite normal, you know.'

But he had preferences. Today, on the tube, he'd leaned towards Ananda when a mildly plump West Indian woman—unmindful, maybe tired—got on at Camden Town and sat opposite them, and said with an evil smile: 'Pupu, I'm feeling some lust for her.' Ananda speculated anxiously if she'd heard. But the hum was in the foreground.

A narrow range preoccupied his uncle on the menu of desire: black and working women. Granted, his love for Gilberta had been more devotion rather than Eros—heartfelt and unsullied (which is why it had brought him pain). But, as a rule, sexual desire and romantic longing were, for his uncle, incompatible with each other. It was one of the reasons, he'd implied, he hadn't married. He'd gone out with refined Bengali women and Englishwomen, but they were only good for attentive walks and conversations about poetry and life. On the other hand, maidservants: they were funny and down-to-earth.

* * *

6

Ithaca

There were no lights on in either Mandy's flat or the Patels'. Ananda's own second-floor windows reflected the sun. Eyes lowered, the neighbours hanging, in a manner of speaking, over his head, Ananda unlocked the door. The morning's clutter had shrunk. They went up, making an extroverted thumping sound. As Ananda attained the first-floor landing, Mandy's door opened and shut again. Maybe she'd wanted to pounce on him about his morning practice and changed her mind. Hold on—she wasn't home. Only the budgies, stoic and immobile. His uncle was humming away in his train—soft, deep voice.

*

Once inside, he went to a window and lifted it further up. The oncoming night was festive and menacing. But it was a moot point whether Tandoor Mahal—the fairy lights around its menu glowing—would get customers. It *had* to. It was Friday. The inside of the flat was in shadow. When he pressed the switch, cushions sprang out of the dark.

215

'Pupu.' His uncle dangled the Budgens bag. 'Keep these in the kitchen.'

'You sure you won't take them home?' asked Ananda hopefully.

'O no no no!' his uncle said, entirely resolved. 'I'd never eat them.' Yes, he *would* finish them, probably single-handed, but only in company; here. Ananda could imagine him dithering over a laddoo in 24 Belsize Park. Laddoos were not, ordinarily, consumed in solitude.

'Keep the bag,' added his uncle.

'You won't need it?'

'O, these bags!' He shrugged, as if it possessed no value. 'I have hundreds.' A treasure trove.

*

In the kitchen, he noticed the smell of his mother's cooking. The kitchen was still but for the fridge's neutral throbbing. A secret place.

Returning to the room, he saw his uncle crouching over last year's books on shelves Ananda and his mother had brought home from Habitat—books whose alienness he'd had to understand and tame and which he was now liberated from. His uncle was examining *Piers Plowman*.

'I haven't heard of this Langland,' he said. 'The English poets we knew of were Milton and Shelley . . . Shelley was the greatest Romantic kobi, wasn't he?' Solemnly he intoned:

'"Let pity clip thy wings before you go."'

'Langland is from much further back.'

'Yes, this doesn't even read like what you and I would take to be English,' said his uncle, frowning and scrutinising the page. 'Too intellectual. Maybe a bit above my head . . .' he said with sly self-deprecation.

'Langland wasn't an intellectual, Rangamama,' said Ananda, bristling. 'At least, I don't think so. To tell you the truth, very little's known about him.'

His uncle lowered himself on to a chair by the dining table. He still hadn't taken off his pinstripe jacket.

'What are *you* reading? I hope you have a decent horror novel at hand?'

'Yes, it's not bad,' replied his uncle casually, placing his right leg on the left knee. 'Also, I'm rereading *Debojan*. Wonderful book! Have you heard of it?' How could Ananda have not? It was a sacred text to his uncle; every other conversation was punctuated by a reference to it. 'It's by Bibhutibhushan Banerjee. You know Bibhutibhushan, of course?' About Bengali literature, his uncle presumed a scandalous ignorance on Ananda's part. Ananda was from a breed on a new planet, impossibly removed from the world that had formed his own parents. That old Bengal that his uncle had left behind, and which was gone forever . . . Ananda in fact knew Bibhutibhushan, who'd written *Pather Panchali*—an unprepossessing man, but a great cherisher and noticer of the everyday, the mundane; he'd had no clue earlier that there was another side to him, which was drawn to the transmigratory.

'What's the book about?' said Ananda, though he'd had pretty intricate accounts before from his uncle.

His uncle was happy to take up the theme again.

'It's highly interesting,' he said, with the air of an anthropologist. 'For instance, he describes the astral plane.'

'What's that exactly?'

'It's a plane much like the one we live on, but where you experience things more intensely. Even a beautiful summer's day like today would be so much more vivid on the astral plane.'

'I see.' Ananda weighed the remark, and tried to conceive how this day's beauty might increase. 'In what way?'

'Things . . . *tremble* on the astral plane.'

He vibrated one hand, like a man who'd been administered a jolt of electricity.

'It's mainly about life after death,' he said, moving on rapidly, unrestrainably. 'The soul journeying through the stars and the cosmos. All sorts of extraordinary things happen on that journey! At a certain point, it can hear the screaming of the souls of various animals that have been slaughtered for our consumption.'

Ananda nodded—as if he could almost hear the dreadful din himself.

'Do you know,' said his uncle, untying his shoelaces, 'that when a man dies he often doesn't know what's happened? It's described in *Debojan*. A man suddenly falls dead on the street, say, or is hit by a car. The body's taken away in an ambulance.

But the soul doesn't realise what's going on. So the man gets up, goes home as usual.' Painfully, he wrested a sneaker off. 'Everything's as it was. A while later, he notices his wife and children are weeping. He thinks: *What's wrong?* He goes to them. But they continue to mourn; they don't seem to notice him. It's at that point that an already dead person might come to him and break the news—and guide him to the other world. He'd be reluctant to go, of course; he might have a daughter to marry, a debt to pay. It's hard to pull away.'

Both sneakers had come off.

'Who would this already-dead person be?' asked Ananda—witnessing, in his head, the disconsolate progression of events.

'Oh it could be anyone. But someone who knows the dead person. Maybe a friend. Or it might be a relation.'

Ananda was soothed by this. He'd never much cared for the conception of the afterlife. Even misery in Warren Street was more congenial to him than any possible idea of paradise. But the thought of being reunited with a known figure who'd keep you company, after your death, on your journey to the hereafter spoke to everything in him that, ever since he could recall, was groping its way through this world.

'Would you be scared if you saw such a—saw someone of that kind?'

'Of course I would!' said his uncle, histrionically enlarging his eyeballs. He scratched his ankle, making a rasping sound. 'I don't want to see a ghost!'

'If it were someone you knew?'

'Even if it were my mother, my dear friend,' he said, absolving himself of being the type that rejoiced upon seeing a phantom. 'I would be—I'd be terrified!'

'Mm,' said Ananda. He switched on the TV and was greeted by a gale of uproarious laughter. Terry and June were in bed, confabulating.

'I had a dream once,' said his uncle, oblivious to the mirth, which had as suddenly subsided. 'You know that when our father died, we three younger ones—Dukhu, your ma Khuku, and I—were reigned over by the three older siblings who had forceful personalities: Chhorda, Sejda, and Didi. Our mother protected and looked over us all, but she had no real influence over us. Mejda was too dreamy. It was these three who controlled us: the committee.' He pursed his lips at the memory of their authority. 'Then Sejda—who sang Tagore songs more beautifully than anyone else I've heard—died at the age of thirty.' He looked at Ananda; Ananda looked back at him, experiencing a sorrow that was distant, yet curiously personal. Ananda had never seen this uncle; he remained forever youthful in these stories; forever in Sylhet in undivided British India. 'We were all completely shattered. Others cried; I grew very quiet. We knew he had a bad heart, but he was so versatile—he baked wonderful cakes, and played the harmonium magnificently (no one taught him, don't know how he picked it up)— that we never expected it to happen.' Further merriment: Terry had emerged awkwardly from bed and was wearing his trousers. 'Two days later, I had a dream.

Sejda had just got back home with a group of English officers he was friendly with. He was sitting in the drawing room—they were talking and laughing loudly. Then Chhorda called me aside and said, "Doesn't he know he can't do that? Why is he sitting over there? Go and tell him he's dead!"' Rangamama sighed. 'He gave *me* that chore—to go and break the news.'

Chhorda, the brother for whom he sent a monthly cheque to Shillong.

'You should read the book,' he said semi-urgently, as if it wasn't too late. 'Can you *read* Bengali?'

'A little,' Ananda confessed.

'It's known everywhere. In China they call it *Deb-chan*.' He spat out the syllables. 'Deb-chan!' he said again, almost making an authentic Chinese sound.

'Rangamama!'

His uncle looked up.

'What are you doing?'

He'd drawn blood. He'd rolled down one sock, and, while endorsing Bibhutibhushan's tale, was mauling an itch.

'Sorry.' A bit sheepish. 'These feet get no air.'

He brushed off the dead skin. 'Do you have the Betnovate C?' he asked, with the incisiveness of a connoisseur.

Ananda's mother had carried two tubes with her for her brother and his longstanding complaint and left them at Warren Street.

Ananda groped among objects on the top shelf of the cupboard adjoining the bed.

221

There was a sound like a thunderclap. Then a drumbeat of footsteps that gathered and grew till there was a bustling transit right past Ananda's flat. After two or three seconds, there was emphatic footfall upstairs.

'Here,' said Ananda, handing over a small green tube.

His uncle squeezed and abstractedly daubed the cream on the raw, pink spot. Ananda couldn't bear to look.

'Aren't you hungry?' asked his uncle, massaging the ankle. 'I could eat a horse!'

*

'Why don't we eat at the Indian YMCA? Their meals are superb . . .'

So *that's* why they were heading for Fitzroy Square! Ananda was resistant to the large breast of chicken in the red YMCA curry, along with sides of daal and vegetables (stubs of beans and carrots) and the heap of white rice. He wanted pilau rice. And maybe the reliable quick fixes, lamb *bhuna* or chicken tikka masala.

'No, Rangamama. Not the YMCA.'

'Why not?' Genuine disbelief at this jettisoning. 'The chicken curry is mouth-watering!'

Not egregious, maybe, but certainly not 'mouth-watering'. And Ananda didn't take to the canteen ethos, irrepressible men in tight suits and wives in salwar kameez congregated in solidarity in tables of six. Oh, he'd forgotten the ice cream:

222

gratifying bonus. Non-veg was just two pounds fifty a head.

'No,' he said.

Fitzroy Square: the outskirts of Bloomsbury. Redolent this time of year. Again, Ananda thought of his mother, her omniscient chatter, her crusades. His uncle and he felt incomplete without her. Why did he miss her? Was it what Sunjay (finalist at LSE, staying upstairs before the Patels came along) had said: 'The reason you want your mother here is because she cooks you nice meals.' How far he'd been from the truth! 'Of course not,' he'd replied at once, but had been unable to explain what her proximity denoted—because it was a recent, and astonishing, discovery for him too. He hadn't been *aware* of his mother as a separate being when he was a child.

The moon was up, but a deeper layer of the sky—under its skin—glowed with the remnants of sunshine. You could hear shouting in the distance. It was best to be careful of revellers. All week, they'd have been set a punitive regime. They'd have curbed every impulse and desire. The shouts now were shouts of freedom. Drink enabled them to find their true voices. Tonight and tomorrow evening they'd wander about, seized by celebrations, hectoring you when they didn't recognise you. Wisest to pretend you hadn't noticed, and give them a long rope to hang themselves with.

'What about here?'

Ali's Curry House.

They'd come full circle, almost. The corner of Whitfield

and Grafton streets: on their right, Diwan-i-Khas, and, on the left, just by the Jamaican record shop (dark now), Ali's. A venerable Pakistani gentleman in a traditional long jacket was pottering about behind troughs filled (hard to guess from when) with a morass of *saag gosht*, a dead pool of chicken curry, daal, and a bank of pilau rice by another basin discreetly crowded with florets of gobi.

'I'm not eating that.'

'Why? It looks marvellous!'

'The last occasion I ate their food—it was with you—I got a stomach upset.'

Mr Ali—if that's who the patient diminutive man was—smiled affectionately from within while presiding over the troughs.

'Well,' said his uncle, 'the English say that Indian food is useful for a good purging.'

If you were reconciled to the curry being a laxative, you could even view it as a variety of health food. Ananda didn't want to dwell on the merits of this argument. They walked a bit further up.

Finally, they relented and entered the restaurant almost next to Walia's, the Gurkha Tandoori. Why it was so called they were uninterested in—nevertheless, the name (and the red wallpaper in the hallway) set up expectations of proud and outdated martial codes.

The restaurant was secreted away in the basement. The moment they'd descended, a waiter greeted them with a

'Table for two?' in a Sylheti accent. Careless with the 'b', pushing *table* close to *te-vul*. Ananda felt he was near home. Not home in Bombay: his parents didn't speak Sylheti in that large-hearted peasant way; their accent was slightly gentrified. Not Warren Street of course. Not Sylhet, either—he'd never been there and didn't particularly regret it. Maybe some notion of Sylhet imparted to him inadvertently by his parents and relations—as an emblem of the perennially recognisable . . . And the perennially comic. Sylhet, and Sylheti, made everybody in his family laugh with joy.

'Yes please,' said Ananda sombrely.

The waiter said, 'Follow me please!' and promptly commandeered the way.

He seated them not too far from a table of thirteen or fourteen people. A vocal, exultant group. Someone would make a remark, another add their bit, and laughter would spread from one end of the table to the other. A few, by turns convulsed by gaiety and introspective, bit into poppadums; some jabbed shards of poppadum into mango chutney. *They are so happy*, thought Ananda. *Why shouldn't they be? It's their country after all. What they do and how they behave is law.* Then: *But are they happy? Sometimes their laughter's like an assault on the surroundings. It's a form of aggression.* His uncle was examining the menu with a faux pedantic air. It was more a performance of menu-reading—he'd leave the actual ordering to Ananda. Ha ha ha ha ha. *They do like a weekly Indian meal, don't they?*

'Sir.'

The dapper waiter.

'Would you like to order?' Now embracing the cockney style. *Oh-dah*. Chameleon.

'Uh yes, thank you.' Ananda turned to his uncle. 'What do you think?'

'Oh let the young man here do the honours. Right?' said his uncle to the Sylheti. 'The young should lead the way!'

The waiter chortled.

'Chicken jhalfrezi?' said Ananda, letting the question hang.

'Jhalfrezi!' said his uncle, with the exaggerated enthusiasm of one who has no clue what his interlocutor's proposing. It was the same principle—over-compensation—that fuelled righteous indignation. 'Mouth-watering!' He'd involuntarily checked the price, and was much enlivened that it wasn't one of the expensive dishes.

'Would you like it hot or less hot?' the waiter asked. 'It is very hot.' An oft-repeated caveat that he clearly relished. He sent forth a surreptitious glance, briefly on tenterhooks for their reply.

'Hot is fine,' said Ananda in a casual-grand way. The waiter nodded, and made a note.

'Daal?' Ananda said. Sooner or later you had to pronounce this word—you could not evade it.

'One tarka daal?' chimed in the waiter, pencil poised, accustomed to being two steps ahead of everyone. He barked the words like a command.

'Oh daal is a must, innit!' agreed Rangamama. He imported colloquialisms in company whenever he became intolerably expansive. Then, realising he was being a nuisance, but admitting to his ineluctable love of the potato, he said, needing the green signal from his nephew, 'Pupu, can't we have potatoes? What is life without potatoes?' Ananda had never been able to figure out his uncle's supplication to the potato; but there was nothing insincere about the light in his eye. 'Bombay potato?' his uncle said.

'Bombay alu?' asked the waiter in return.

'Please,' said Ananda. Be done with it.

'Would you like naan bread or pilau rice?'

'Pilau rice,' replied Ananda gravely—it was the inevitable choice. Driven by obscure racial characteristics handed down over millennia, Bengalis might flirt with bread but succumb, at the end of the day, to rice.

After issuing a cheery 'Thank you!', about to race off like a man whose real job was about to begin, the waiter checked himself: 'Would you like some poppadums?' Ananda and his uncle contemplated each other; Ananda was no great fan of the poppadum, but it was graceless to admit this. 'Not really, don't think so.'

The waiter hurried away. In the meanwhile, trolleys of food had been navigated towards the boisterous table nearby.

'Wonder if it's a birthday party?' said Ananda, glancing at the multiple vessels of curry and the effervescent grilled platters. 'Quite a banquet. I wish they wouldn't make such a racket!'

'Oh they're all right!' His uncle made it a point to be magnanimous when Ananda was carping. In retaliation, Ananda plotted to be equable or indifferent when his uncle carped, but forgot each time to execute the plan. 'They're just living it up a bit!' Living it up! Clichés that his uncle plucked from the air according to his mood.

'I can't stand the English—especially when they're being sociable,' whispered Ananda.

Two small men were holding pans above blonde and brown-haired heads that almost came up to their shoulders.

'Oh they're human too!' his uncle said with some conviction. 'And,' here he very sadly expressed a historical truth that he knew might wind Ananda up, 'they *do* belong to what used to be the "master race".' At other times, when it suited him, he'd argue otherwise, saying that Europeans, with their blues eyes that were discomfited by the sun and their rapacious history, were suspiciously 'different'. 'By the way, English women can be very kind—much kinder than Bengali women.'

'They *may* be kind,' said Ananda. Neither Hilary Burton nor the Anglo-Saxon teacher had struck him as particularly *kind*. He'd sensed a sweetness in one or two of the girls in college he'd never had the time or will to talk to—mooning as he fruitlessly was over his cousin. 'But for some reason the English emanate unpleasantness in groups. You see a bunch of Englishmen talking loudly on the tube and you feel uncomfortable—even threatened. If it's some loud Italians, you don't really notice them.'

'That's to do with drink,' said his uncle. 'There's an unwritten law in this land that you can't criticise drinking. All the propaganda—the surgeon-general's health warning etcetera—is about smoking.' He spoke bitterly. When Ananda first met him, he'd smoke serially, with little self-consciousness or sense of apology. Then, despite his defiance of the dark anti-smoking conspiracy, the 'propaganda' must have got to him, because he'd defected to Silk Cut, which was low-tar. His smoking was petering out. Today, despite the stub floating in the toilet in Belsize Park, Ananda hadn't actually *seen* him smoke a cigarette. 'They keep saying smoking kills you. It's a lie. What they won't say is that drinking is far more lethal than smoking—and it changes the personality too.'

In response, a cheer went up at the big table. His uncle, distracted by the mood, clapped his hands in glee. Someone glanced back for a second.

'What are you *doing*?' asked Ananda.

'Just joining in,' said his uncle. 'Everyone's feeling jolly.'

Ananda shook his head in reproach at this disloyalty.

'It's certainly not Christmas,' he said. 'And it doesn't seem to be anyone's birthday either—or they'd have been singing by now.'

In fact, they were soon quieter, making a hubbub as they ate.

The waiter appeared with a plate of poppadums. Poppadum after poppadum had floated down, settling on top of each other, making a low tower. 'On the house!' he said.

Ananda felt an onrush of emotion. 'Thank you!' He was tempted to communicate—to share their common ancestry. But he held back. Maybe the waiter had guessed, or had some half-formed inkling? He was no fool.

'*My* birthday,' his uncle snapped a bit of the poppadum off (the conversation had to veer round at some point to the enduring theme: himself), 'falls on a particularly unlucky day.'

'13th June?' Ananda recalled it well. Last month, his mother had stood before the cooker and, over an hour, reduced a pan of milk to produce rice payesh for her 'dada'—a delicate thing, almost unbearably sweet, such as both she and his uncle preferred. But he'd orchestrated a terrible quarrel on the phone—punishing her for her old and recent transgressions, including the mistake she'd made in confiding in Basanta in Pinner, and possibly for even having the temerity to marry Satish at all. Those deeds couldn't be undone. But it was his birthday. She'd transferred some of the payesh to a bowl, covered it with a saucer, tied the whole makeshift arrangement with a cloth, and, to Ananda's chagrin, carried it via the tube and road to Belsize Park. 'He's a vagabond,' she'd soothed Ananda. 'You can't take his rages seriously.'

'Not just 13th June!' said his uncle in a pained hypochondriac's tone. '*Friday* the 13th. My birthday. The unluckiest day of the year.' A shout was released from the other table as someone made a little speech.

'What's wrong with thirteen?' asked Ananda. 'Baba always says thirteen is his lucky number. You know his roll number was thirteen when he appeared for his Chartered Accountancy exams. And he passed!'

His father: a foil to his wife and his best friend. Tranquil and moored.

'Your father!' His uncle shook his head fondly.

Coming out of nowhere, the waiter shouted: 'Tarka daal!' What joy! The evening's climax! Nothing—not even the eating—could match the festive instant of the order materialising. 'One pilau rice!' Retrieving more from the trolley, he continued: 'One jhalfrezi! One Bombay alu!' A pause. 'All right?'

'My goodness, this is fit for a king!'

'*Khub bhalo*,' said Ananda. '*Dhanyabad*.'

The waiter seemed not to hear the Bengali words—he stood beside the table, congenial and undecided.

'*Apnar naam?*' asked Ananda.

'Iqbal,' said the man, a bit guarded.

'Wonderful name! A very famous poet—Iqbal!' said his uncle. He then emptied half the platter of the pilau rice on to his plate—red, white, and yellow grains, perfumed with cloves, cinnamon, and cardamom, a few possibly stiffened by the microwave's heat. 'Pupu, have some!' He must be starving—Ananda had heard his stomach bubbling—but he was serving himself with considerable discipline. He wouldn't start until he'd cajoled Ananda into having an inaugural mouthful.

'Some jhalfrezi?' Iqbal said. He'd picked up a serving dish with alacrity.

'We Bengalis,' said his uncle in standard Calcutta Bangla, 'eat course by course—I have no idea why. *I* like mixing things up. Pupu, what are you doing, have some Bombay alu!'

In prelapsarian undivided Bengal, as his uncle had once revealed wryly to Ananda, the Bengali Hindus were called 'Bengalis', the Bengali Muslims just 'Muslims'.

Iqbal was vaguely nonplussed.

'Are you gentlemen from Calcutta?' he asked politely.

'I'm from India,' said Ananda. 'But my parents were from Sylhet. This is my uncle—he was born in Sylhet.'

He lifted up a spoonful: the daal was incredible—a ghee and garlic-infused ambrosia.

Iqbal studied Ananda's uncle, who appeared to be rotating the food in his mouth in dilatory contentment.

'Which part of Sylhet are you from?' He'd switched to Sylheti—always charming to hear: this fluent, rapid, and intimate tongue.

'Habiganja,' replied his uncle serenely, having just swallowed. 'We grew up in Sylhet town—in Puran Lane when we were small, then mostly in Lamabajar.' Being a Tagorean, he refused to answer him in the rustic tongue of his childhood, but addressed him in a slightly affected Bengali, trying (as usual) to disguise the East Bengali inflection he'd never be rid of. Gesturing to Ananda, he volunteered grandly: 'My sister's son. Can you tell?'

'Habiganja!' said Iqbal, not attending to this last query. 'I know Habiganja . . . and Lamabajar!' He smiled reminiscently.

'Who are they?' asked Ananda, with a conspiratorial tipping of his head towards the table of fourteen. 'Sounds like they're celebrating tonight.'

'Oh them!' said Iqbal. He kept his eyes off the table. 'Those kind of people come every Friday night for "curry".' He used the word fastidiously, as a pejorative. 'They drink too much.' He spoke with patrician distaste while dispassionately spectating on Ananda and his uncle eating.

*

When it came to the tip, Ananda felt duty-bound to curtail his uncle. For his uncle had an incurable tipping problem. The trouble was, his uncle acted in consultation. 'Three pounds?' 'That's crazy,' said Ananda. With the gulab jamun that was their final excess (his uncle had asked Iqbal to heat his up, and, after masticating the pincushion-like sweet whole, had tippled the syrup from the chalice), the bill had come to ten pounds thirty. 'That's almost thirty per cent.' 'It's a generous tip.' 'I know you're rich,' said Ananda, 'but you shouldn't distribute your bounty indiscriminately.' His uncle frowned, paralysed, a wad of notes in his hand. (He didn't deny he was wealthy.) Scrutinising the bill, they found the total smaller than it should have been as Bombay Potato had inexplicably been omitted. They beckoned to the waiter. 'There's been a mistake,' said Ananda. The other waved one hand in dismissal of an imaginary trifle. 'Bombay Potato is on the house.'

*

Stomachs heavy, they walked down Whitfield Street. Confronting, in a few minutes, the building on Warren Street, Ananda studied it as if it were a dark castle. No lights on the first, second, and top floors. They stepped in. Almost at once, a rumbling sound. The Patels were hurtling down the stairs. A brief arrest as they saw each other. Ananda continued up the stairs, but his uncle, hamming it up, said: 'Vivek! How are you? And this handsome young man is your brother, isn't he?' As Ananda entered the flat, he heard laughter. The words, 'I'm a black Englishman,' seemed to float eerily up the staircase.

*

By the time his uncle came in, Ananda was cross-legged on the sofa, grinning at *Rising Damp*. He didn't care when the Patels and Mandy would make their entrance again. His spirits were high. Poetry, at this moment, couldn't do the job (not Edward Thomas, not Larkin) that Leonard Rossiter was doing so expertly, exuding an obtuse grandeur.

Standing before him, marginally blocking his view, his uncle said: 'Could you change the channel? There's too much laughter on television. People are dying in various parts of the world, but in this culture you have to have something to laugh at.' He narrowed his eyes, awaiting a rebuke for his sermon.

But there were more squeals as Leonard Rossiter, updating the African tenant Don Warrington on English etiquette, stole a glimpse of Frances de la Tour's cleavage.

With admirable self-control, Ananda, eyes on the small lit screen, said: 'It's hilarious, Rangamama. You may enjoy it.'

His uncle looked pained and at sea.

'But I prefer tragedy to comedy, Pupu.'

By 'tragedy' his uncle meant B-grade action movies— that is, a narrative with dead bodies. Comedy alienated him because he neither followed jokes nor had the patience to stay with them till the punchline. He was terribly inattentive. His consciousness was too fluid to have a grasp on a story from start to end. How he'd shone at exams was a mystery. In action films, too, he had no time for plot and was placated as long as periodic killings occurred. The last action film he'd fully comprehended and cogitated on was probably *High Noon*. Given the story wasn't the point, he could plunge into an adventure at any juncture—even midway through a movie. The occasional calamity kept him quiet.

'Or you could check if they're showing wildlife! We could be missing the tiger, Pupu!'

This was a recurrent addiction—to gawp awestruck the

great beasts in Africa, while they lolled, napped, sunned themselves, blinked at distant cameras, then pursued and devoured the lesser and stupider animals.

'There are no wildlife programmes at this hour,' Ananda assured him. 'Sit down.'

Reluctantly—as if he'd rather walk a few more miles—he descended on the sofa. He began to loosen his shoelaces. Let those ankles breathe. Reaching impatiently for the remote control—he was hopeless with devices, but now had the measure of this one—he pushed both himself and Ananda into a vortex of channel-changing. Finally, calming down, he laid the remote control on the sofa, and said:

'I've eaten too much.'

Tamely, in accidental concord, they'd come back to laughter and *Rising Damp*.

'Do you want a laddoo?' Ananda was under pressure to dispense with six uneaten ones.

His uncle gave him an eloquent stare.

'Are you mad? Do you want me to die tonight?'

Though lazy and recumbent for now, he'd be off to Belsize Park in twenty minutes. What an idiotic plan Ananda had had once—that they'd *share* that bedsit. Not because it was too small. But you couldn't share *any* space with him: to live with his uncle would be to go mad. Or at least to be changed; or sidetracked permanently, indubitably, from a traditional idea of coexistence. No wonder God, in his mercy, had withheld a spouse from him.

236

'In fact, I'm going to put on weight as a result of that *slap-up meal*,' he complained. 'Anyway, my cheeks have always been too fat and my face too round.' Ananda glanced quickly away from Frances de la Tour to confirm that his uncle was describing the person he knew. While it may not have met Rangamama's standards of consumptive narrowness, the face wasn't round at all; the cheeks weren't full. Yet the baritone had a way of casting a spell which meant almost everything his uncle uttered sounded true and reasonable. Half the time you argued with him not to dispute him but to fend off becoming an accomplice to his vision. 'Also, my nose becomes larger when I eat too much.' Just as Ananda prepared to debate the canonical European preference for starved, phalange-like noses, his uncle observed: 'You know that a large nose is a sign of virility.'

'Is it?' Given that Ananda had grown up in the world essentially in the proximity of a mother who talked unstoppably, he was quite capable of following *Rising Damp* and engaging in a dialogue with his uncle simultaneously. As they slipped into a commercial break, he let himself relax and consider these questions. The nose and virility: he speculated on the kind of equation being made here. It was vaguely obvious. But what reliable knowledge would a virgin have of virility? Intriguingly, experience didn't seem to matter so much when it came to Ananda's uncle. He always sounded more experienced than he could possibly be. As if he had recourse to some other source of information outside reading, education, and life.

'Oh very much so. You know that Christ had a big nose?'

Not that Christ was particularly celebrated for his virility. Still, Ananda found this an arresting piece of information. He hadn't known that there were actual likenesses available—which could have attested to the feature. The Roman Catholic portrait at the reception of the Indian YMCA displayed the generic Christ, the timorous, blonde-haired, blue-eyed face upturned to the heavens, a lost middle-class student searching for guidance in an inhospitable world.

'If you think Christ looked the way they show him in films,' said his uncle, gazing straight at Ananda, as if he'd caught him out indulging in exactly such an irresponsible misconception, 'you'd be wrong. Christ wasn't European: he was from the Middle East. It is said that he had a large prominent nose. The way you see him today is Western propaganda.'

He leaned back on the sofa, unarguable, his nose radiating a new power, looking like he was in no hurry to leave. The next moment he got up.

'Small job,' he clarified.

He shuffled off to the neighbouring bathroom.

A thunderclap. The Patels. Or was it Mandy? Back earlier than expected. Ananda steeled himself. Another bang—below him. Mandy. You had to feel for her, actually. Solitary homecomings. From Paul Hogan draining a can of lager in the outbacks—such were the images (caricatures of epic voyages) that flashed before you as the day drew to a close—Ananda looked behind him at Warren Street, the pale torches of the speaking of? For was the shudra anywhere near finding dignity and freedom? It seemed not. Then in what way the age of the shudra? Unless it was some allegory he meant . . . Of course—*then* it made sense, as an insane cosmogony. The caste system could serve as a metaphor for the epochs succeeding each other since the dawn of time. Ananda was momentarily happy to go along with the scheme. The first age, of Brahman, was (decided Ananda proudly) India's—the Brahman not being the pusillanimous priest with the sacred thread, but the spiritual man, who could have any provenance whatsoever, emerge from any caste: the sage and renunciate. The second age, of the Kshatriya, the warriors and aristocrats, was Rome's. The king and the notion of Empire was then supreme. It was the aristocrat who fostered and nurtured value and beauty and the arts. When the aristocracy went to seed the third age came into being, of the Vaishya—the merchant. You *had* to grant that epoch to the English: the ascendancy and rule of the shopkeeper, the burgher, who might possess an Empire but whose outlook was essentially humdrum, middle-level, and suburban. (Amazing how the allegory fell into place.) Finally, the last age: the shudra's—in which the man on the street was illusorily empowered. (For power invariably deceives those it passes on to.) It was a toss-up whether—if you subscribed to the metaphor—the epoch belonged to Russia or America. It would seem America. For this would be the epoch nominally of the common man, but really of capitalism and popular culture. Everyone would be famous. And after this final phase (Ananda hoped it would take another century to truly arrive)—what?

'Pupu.'

Ananda looked up.

'It's after eleven . . . I'd better head off before the tube closes.'

Yet another outing! Could he be sprightly, setting out now for Belsize Park? At least it was warm. Better than those chill nights on which he'd dutifully make his way homeward from his nephew. Ananda nodded, briefly and fiercely hating the peace and quiet that came at the end of everything. Mandy was very still, as if she were in hiding. Yet be grateful for the peace before the Patels are back again—and for this indecisive lull before his uncle declaims on a detail he'd forgotten about in his rush to depart. He was loitering: clearly not about to say goodbye just yet. *Never say, 'I'm leaving.' Always, 'I'll be seeing you.'* '"*Jachhi*" *bolte nei*, Pupu, but "*aschhi*".'

'So—do I see you on Monday then?' enquired Ananda of the hovering figure.

Acknowledgements

I'm fortunate to have the belief and support of a group of great readers who also happen to be my agent and publishers: Peter Straus, Chiki Sarkar, Rosalind Porter, Sonny Mehta, Diana Miller.

My mother continues, as ever, to inspire me: this book is for her too.

Rinka embraced the idea when I put it to her: I procrastinated, and she brought me round.

Lastly, there's Radha, to whom I am grateful for—among other things—thinking I am funny.